he loves me

Also by Carmen Rosales

Erotic Quill Publishing, LLC
3020 NE 41st Terrace STE 9 #243
Homestead, Fl. 33033
www.carmenrosales.com

Manufactured in the United States of America

First Edition November 2023

To all the girls and boys who played a game of he loves me, he loves me not and arrived at love.

Even when he they hated you.

To my husband Junior,
I couldn't write without you.

Acknowledgments

He Loves me and He Loves Me Not is a special story about young love and the lengths we will go to hold on to that special person in our hearts. Even though it has a fictional twist and brushes on hard topics, we all have that special boy or girl we fell in love with in our hearts.

I would like to thank my readers, book bloggers, and Arc readers for your time, patience and support. I could not have done this without you.

To Melissa, thank you for a beautiful cover. I also would like to thank my family for giving me the support to live my dream. To my PR team, thank you for your time and for all the hard work you all put in marketing my books. I will be forever grateful to you all.

AUTHOR's NOTE

He Loves Me is book two and is part of a duet. You must read He Loves Me Not in order to read He Loves Me. It is a dark high school romance. The list of triggers include depression, death, acts of violence, acts of bullying, mental illness, and suicidal thoughts.

He Loves Me also contains sex scenes that is consensual for the enjoyment of all parties involved. It is intended for mature audiences and is not suitable for all readers. Reader discretion is advised. If you are comfortable, please move forward and enjoy.

If you or know anyone you know that is suffering from mental health and needs help. Please call *National Suicide Prevention Lifeline in your local area.*

*All good things that come to an end make way for new beginnings.
Even in the shadow of past deceptions, even when forbidden.*

Rubi grapples with Ky's unrelenting hate, finding herself
ensnared in the perilous intricacies of his life. She discovers he
doesn't seek to break her but to own her completely.

When Ky uncovers the secrets Rubi has harbored for years, his
heart shatters once more. He's determined to right his wrongs,
but an invisible barrier keeps them apart, and trust is a fragile
commodity. Ky must confront his true self to rescue the girl who
possesses his heart.

Obsession breeds madness, and she's... his fixation.

he loves me

BOOK TWO

CARMEN ROSALES

Prologue
RUBI

I'M in the car with Ky, and he hasn't said a word since we left the house. He made sure the window was left in a way that was easy to get back inside. I guess that is how he has been able to get in and out of my room. The cabin of the car is quiet, and it feels like the silence is going to strangle me, but when I look at the screen of the dash, there are so many buttons, I'm not sure what to press to play some music.

I pull out my phone so it can give me something to do while he drives to who knows where. I'm about to scroll through my social media when he presses the screen and "Angels Fall" by Breaking Benjamin begins to play. He reaches behind to the back seat without swerving and hands me a bag.

"I got this for you." I open the bag and I notice there is a jean skater skirt. I glance at him, and he says, "Put it on."

"Why?"

"Because we're going to play a game."

"What if I don't want to play? What does playing a game have anything to do with wearing a skirt?"

I look up and notice we are back at the fair. The lights shining bright from the rides moving, swinging people around. The parking lot is still full of cars. You can hear the screams of people from a distance. There are lines of people in the front buying tickets.

He turns his head with a hard glint in his eyes. "A game I want to play with you, Rubi. It is part of the game. Like a uniform. Since you have such a hard time listening to what I tell you to do.

1

This is the way I will make you understand. I brought you back here because we are going to play a game called twenty-two rides."

Twenty-two rides? I have never heard of it, but there are many things I haven't heard of and I'm curious. What does that game have to do with the fair and wearing a jean skirt?

"I have never heard of that game?"

He leans close and looks down at my thighs, slowly trailing until he reaches my mouth. "Put the skirt on, Rubi."

I sigh and look around but remember that his windows are tinted pitch black. I unbutton my jeans and lift my ass to slide them off. He doesn't move, watching me fumble with the bag and the skirt. I slide the skirt over my thighs, and notice it is a tad short, but I think that was his intention.

"You have pretty thighs, Rubi. I'm going to love dirtying them."

I suck in a breath when his lips are an inch from mine. His hand slides up my thighs until they are in the center of my panties under the skirt. The tip of his finger ghosting the fabric where my clit is throbbing to be touched.

"Ky," I whisper, the movement causing my lips to brush delicately against his.

"Open your legs, *preciosa*. I want to see how wet you are for me."

His mouth crashes against mine, and a whimper escapes my lips. The tip of his finger pinches my clit over my panties as I gasp in his mouth.

"Hmm," he hums. His tongue swirling with mine.

I'm on fire.

I arch my back desperate for more but he releases my clit. Feeling the loss, I grind my hips, seeking more. I want him to fuck me with his fingers. My hands slide in the soft strands of his black hair, getting lost in his kiss. Getting lost in him.

"Please," I hiss.

I moan when his slides my panties to the side and glides a finger over my slit. He doesn't stop kissing me. He slides in the first finger, and I open my legs shamelessly so he can sink in deeper.

"Yes," I moan.

"I'm going to make you come so many times, Rubi."

"Please," I plead going out of my mind.

I'm past feeling ashamed. I want to feel. I want to come so bad my body is betraying my mind telling me to stop. But my body likes what he does to me physically.

He chuckles. "There she is. Don't worry, baby. I'm going to break you some more and you're going to like it. Beg for it."

I hope this isn't a cruel joke and that he doesn't hurt me. He slides in a second finger, stretching me. "Fuck, you're so tight."

My pussy clenches his fingers as my orgasm builds. His lips slide down my jaw to my neck, and he sucks and nibbles on the skin, probably leaving more marks I will have to explain how I got them. He bites and I gasp. "Let go, baby. I'll catch you."

I come hard, but he quickly slides his fingers out and I instantly feel the loss. He picks something up. It is small and shaped like a bullet, and before I can protest, he slides it into my pussy.

I gasp. "What are you doing?"

He smiles, making sure it's seated inside me. When he is done, he lifts his hand to his mouth and licks his fingers. It is sexy watching his tongue savoring me. "What do you think I'm doing? We are playing my game now."

My gut flips, making my nerves and thighs tremor. My heart pounds inside my chest, unease sliding into me when I glance around. He pulls my chin to face him, and I can smell my arousal on his fingers. My emotions are flipping upside down like a coin swirling around to see which side it is going to land.

He then picks up a remote and it has buttons on it. He presses it. A vibration begins inside my pussy causing electric currents to shoot up my clit. My breaths are coming out fast and it feels good. My cheeks grow hot when he presses the button again, increasing the vibration that also causes the pressure to build. It is almost painful, but delicious at the same time.

3

"Please," I beg.

He shuts it off and hands me a hoodie. "Put this on...it might get cold out," he says quietly.

He opens the driver's side door to get out, pressing the button to shut the car off. "You're taking me back to the fair?"

He leans down, giving me a devilish smile. "How did you think I was going to make you scream, Rubi?" He bites his bottom lip. "This is going to be fun. Oh, and don't run, because I'll find you. Starting tonight, you will understand that there is nothing you can do to get rid of me."

"You're crazy. You don't own me, Ky. If I want to leave, I'll leave."

He shakes his head slowly. "But that's just it, Rubi. I have always been crazy. You think you have to keep the monsters out by locking your door and hiding in the closet. What if I told you the only monster you have under your bed is me."

I lean back in the seat of the car. "You're talking psycho again."

But, I let him kiss me, bite me, and fuck me with his fingers, even allow him to slide a bullet-sized vibrator in my pussy knowing that he has a remote. He shuts the door and walks around the car and opens mine, grabbing me by the arm so I have no choice to get out. He slams the door shut with a thud and pushes me up against the car.

His forehead presses against mine, our noses almost touching. Panic begins to squeeze my stomach. "Let me see if I can make myself clear for you so that you understand. Your soul is not safe. Your mind is not safe. You are not safe."

What is he talking about? What does he mean, I am not safe. Am I safe at the house? With him?

He brushes his lips near my ear. Awareness creeping down my throat. If I run, I know he will catch me. And then what? He will just show up. One thing I have noticed, Tyler says to stay away from him, but he doesn't do anything about it. No one does. Ky wants to fuck with me because he knows he can. He wants to play. So, let's play. But his next words has fear gripping me in its embrace. Like shadows dancing, warning me it's too late to back out. Telling me it's too late to run away.

I feel his breath ghosting my skin near my ear. We must look like lovers in a passionate embrace right before we head into the fair. I close my eyes, and his words travel inside me, wreaking havoc within. "I have watched you at night, Rubi. When you think no one is watching. When you think no one is there. You like to sleep in the closet, leaving a crack in the door so you can see what is there in the dark, but if you keep watching long enough, you will eventually see what you should be afraid of. Me."

"What are you talking about?"

Fear is clawing within me. He watches me. It isn't that he just shows up and puts me to sleep.

"I have been watching you the whole time." He rolls his forehead over mine. "Since the first day you arrived, and there is nothing you can do to stop me. So, be a good girl, and let's see how loud you scream." He kisses me, and the darkness in his eyes I remember seeing when we were kids is present. "It is not how you create fear, Rubi. It's how you release it to save the ones you love."

CHAPTER ONE
RUBI

WAITING in line to go on the first ride, all I can think about is the vibrator he slid inside me. I'm already wet in anticipation but scared all at the same time. When we were kids, I felt excitement. I felt whole. Nothing mattered except the next time I would get to see him. But this version of Ky is terrifying. Maybe I knew this part of him was inside, waiting to come out. The way his eyes would always go dark when he would look at me.

The ride attendant unhooks the chain to let the next group on to the ride. Ky pulls my hand, helps me in the seat, and buckles me in before sliding next to me.

The ride lifts in the air like a suspended merry-go-round. My heart is pounding in my ears, knowing the vibrator is between my legs, rubbing every time I'm thrown against Ky's hard body from the force of the ride.

He squeezes my hand under the bar. "Don't worry, Rubi," he says, his voice catching in the wind. "After tonight, you'll never forget coming to the fair." And I believe him.

The ride takes flight, swinging us in the air. My stomach dips, and then the buzzing around my clit starts.

"Oh, my God." I gasp, gripping the bar. My eyes go wide from the buzzing sensation rubbing over my clit.

My nipples begin to ache. I clench my thighs, but it only makes the vibration stronger. Every nerve ending between my thighs is stretched tight, and it's not from the ride, but it feels so good.

I moan between the screams that escape my throat. I feel his hand squeezing my thigh. I arch in the seat against the restraints, grinding my hips shamelessly, seeking my release.

The ride swings us in the air one last time, and I come hard on a scream, making a mess between my legs, the buzzing of the vibrator drawing out my orgasm until I'm spent.

When the ride slows down to a stop, he slides his hand between my thighs under my skirt and presses his fingers over my soaked panties.

"That's how I like you, Rubi. Messy."

Embarrassment grips me because my thighs are sticky and wet. I came all over the bottom part of the skirt, and I'm sure the seat is also damp.

When he helps me off the ride, I look up, and he is sporting a victorious grin. There is no way I could endure another orgasm on another ride.

"I need to go to the bathroom," I tell him when we exit the platform.

"To pee or clean up?" He asks, dragging me along to the next ride.

I pause, pulling my arm out from his grasp. "Ky?"

He arches a brow. "Pee or clean up?" He repeats.

I've never had an orgasm like that before. I've never had a vibrator up my pussy. I'm soaked and shamelessly want more of what, I don't know. I don't need to pee. Not yet, anyway, so I tell him the truth.

"Clean up."

He looks behind me for a second like he's contemplating. "That can be arranged." He pulls me to the house of mirrors.

Again?

But I'm relieved he isn't taking me on another ride. I let him guide me toward the entrance, wondering why is he taking me there if I asked to clean up.

The house is built like a maze. I watch the people in front of me banging themselves on the head for walking the wrong way, wincing from the impact with a smile on their faces like a bunch of idiots.

Ky holds our hands up to show the unlimited band to the ride attendant wrapped around our wrists. The guy looks like he hasn't showered in weeks and nods, allowing us to enter.

Ky goes first, walking through the maze with me in tow. The reflection of my flushed face mocks me in every mirror as he makes his way through the tight space, knowing every turn like the back of his hand.

"Why are we here? What kind of game are we playing, Ky?"

He doesn't answer, pulling me to the left through a large red sheet at the back of the maze, covering a dark space in a corner like a curtain. He pushes me into a dark alcove that isn't part of the maze where two mirrors face each other against each wall. There is some hidden meaning behind the house of mirrors because it is the second time he has taken me here. There is nothing Ky does that doesn't have a purpose.

He pins me against one of the mirrors. "You said you needed to be cleaned up."

"Is this where you bring all your girls this time of year? You seem to know it well."

I sound jealous, but I'm trying to figure him out. Why the change of heart? Why now?

He feels me tense when he slides his hands between my thighs, the tips of his fingers grazing the vibrator lodged inside me. "Damn, you're wet," he says, licking his lips. "Relax, baby," he rasps against my cheek, pulling the vibrator out. "You're the only one." My tummy flutters, but I feel a void build between my legs.

He holds it up, watching him place it in his mouth, holding my gaze, watching him suck it clean. It's sexy and dirty.

"Mm––" he closes his eyes briefly––"you taste so good, Rubi."

My pulse beats widely, watching his tongue lick his lips after he pockets the vibrator in his jeans.

"Look behind me." My eyes shift, finding my reflection in the mirror. "Don't take your eyes off that mirror."

9

Before I get to ask why, he kneels and lifts my skirt, pulling my panties roughly to the side, pressing his lips on my pussy. I gasp when I feel his wet tongue on my sensitive clit. He hooks my leg over his shoulder. A little moan escapes my throat when his tongue trails down to my inner thighs licking me clean.

"Ky," I breathe, holding the side of the metal from the mirror behind me. My eyes watch him between my thighs from the reflection of the mirror. He snakes one hand around my ass, holding me steady while he mauls my pussy with his tongue.

My fingers find his hair with one hand, and I pull. "Mm...Ky," I whimper, feeling another orgasm crest. My leg begins to shake. "I'm coming....I'm...coming," I gasp through a moan, watching myself come apart on his tongue.

I'm so fucked. I'm trying not to beg because that would mean I'm giving in. If I give in to Ky, he will ruin me. This is not the boy whispering innocent things and telling me his dreams when he grows up. This is a man with darkness swirling in the depths of his eyes, waiting to destroy, and right now, his attention is on me.

I can't trust Ky.

I can't trust anyone.

But I feel alive.

When he licks me clean with his tongue, he releases my panties, removes my leg hoisted over his shoulder, and stands up with a gleam in his eye, his mouth glistening.

"You're a mess," I whisper.

He leans in and takes my lips so I can taste myself.

It's different.

I've never tasted myself before. His tongue is hot, and his mouth is needy.

A little whimper escapes my throat when he breaks the kiss.

"Now we are both clean. Our little game is just beginning. Every ride we go on, you will wonder if I want you to come or not." He pulls out the vibrator from his pocket. "I'll have control of your pussy. How many times you can come."

There is no way.

"Ky, I can't--"

He pushes it back inside me, and I mewl. "You're going to tremble, and you're going to beg. I will break you, Rubi, and you'll like it."

I shake my head. "I can't come anymore, Ky. I can't––"

"You can. You just don't know it yet."

CHAPTER TWO
RUBI

"DID YOU LIKE THE FAIR?" Abby asks.

I close my locker, turning to face her, a blush staining my cheeks, remembering Ky's words that night. After I came three more times, and it was time to leave, I passed out in his car from exhaustion. He won me a bigger bear than the one I had when I was there with Chris. I was surprised at how tender he was after. How soft he held me in his arms when he took me home. He helped me climb back into my room like I weighed nothing.

I walked like a zombie to my bed. All I remember is him cleaning me up with a small wet towel before sleep claimed me.

The rest of the weekend, I couldn't stop thinking about what he did or said. The dark expression when he looked at the bear Chris had won for me at the fair.

"Yeah, I had a great time with Chris."

But it was nothing compared to when I went with Ky.

Abby smiles. She likes me hanging out with Chris. But as quickly as that thought passes, Ky appears right behind Abby.

His gaze holds mine. "How was your date at the fair? Did you scream when you went on the rides?" He asks with a knowing grin.

Did he hear?

Abby glances nervously at Ky and then back at me.

I smile, letting him know he doesn't intimidate me. "I wasn't on a date, and yes, I screamed on the scary ones."

He chuckles. Abby steps back so that Ky and I are facing each other. She glances between me and Ky probably wondering why I'm not cowering in front of him and playing it cool.

He crosses his arms across his broad chest and leans his shoulder against the locker. "My favorite is the house of mirrors"––his face grows serious––"do you want to know why?"

Shit.

"Why?" I challenge.

His eyes are hard like a storm in the dark sky, waiting for a flash of lightning. "Because when you walk in the myriad of mirrors, it gives multiple misleading impressions, it adds to the confusion. By the time the scheme of confusion is uncovered, the lies become a maze. Every turn, you wonder if it's the truth or the lie." A chill runs up the middle of my back.

I watch Abby swallow nervously and glance down the hall. "I gotta go."––her eyes meet mine with a wry smile–– "I'm going to be late to class."

The warning bell rings. The throng of bodies skitter down the halls like roaches when the light turns on.

"Yeah, me too," I tell her quietly, trying to hold in the anger from Ky's words. *He's messing with my head. It meant nothing.*

I glare at him in anger when Abby leaves. "I'm a game to you, aren't I?" I move to walk past him and turn around, walking backward. "Stay the fuck away from me, Ky."

He rubs his thumb over his lip. "What would be the fun in that?"

Walking into class, I mutter, "Bastard."

When I sit, I keep looking at the classroom door, expecting Ky to walk through it, but he doesn't.

The door opens, and the teacher walks in, and I don't know if I should be relieved or worried.

After my second class, he still doesn't show up. Is he still in school?

When lunchtime rolls around, I walk into the cafeteria, taking note that Patrick is sitting three tables down, still avoiding me. I can't blame him. Not after Ky threatened him.

Sitting at an empty table, I feel my phone vibrate in my pocket. I pull it out and unlock the screen.

Ky: If you're hungry for some real food, come to the football field.

"Where are you going?" I hear Tyler's voice when I walk past the jock's table on my way out.

I turn, facing him and his friends seated at the table. "What do you care?" I look around mockingly. "Where's Amber?"

I hate how he made Abby feel that night at the fair. I'm not sure what is going on between them, but she was hurt. And I know how it feels to be hurt by someone you like. Someone you care about, and it's out of your control.

He scoffs. "Really? You, too."

That means Abby is giving him the same treatment. I stayed in my room and avoided Tyler all weekend. On the ride to school, I gave him curt responses and made sure I had my headphones on to avoid conversation.

I roll my eyes and walk away. "Rubi!" He calls out, but I ignore him, making my way to the football field.

When I walk outside, squinting against the blinding light of the sun, I spot Ky sitting on the bleachers under the shade as the branches of the tree sway against the light breeze.

He spots me as I walk closer. "Took you long enough," he says, looking straight at me with a pair of black aviators.

I climb the metal bleachers, hearing them clank as I make my way up to the top, where he sits with a box of pizza and two sodas. The smell of cheesy goodness makes my stomach groan when I notice it's the kind I like.

"I like to make you wait. You're lucky I came out after what you said this morning." My stomach makes another whirling sound, hoping he didn't hear it.

"Hungry?" He asks with a smirk.

Shit, was it that loud?

I plop myself next to him under the shade and open the box. Steam lifts off the cheese, and I feel like I'm in heaven. All the previous anger I had for him for what he said this morning evaporated into thin air. It's the New York-style kind I love. The cheese melted on the thin crust with light red sauce.

I break a slice off, handing him the first feeling butterflies swarm in my stomach when his fingers brush against my hand.

He sits up when he takes it from me. "Let's see what the big deal is about this pizza."

I lift my brow in challenge. "It's the best." I pick up another slice taking a bite. And groan, rolling my eyes when the warm cheesy goodness hits my tongue.

It tastes so good–– anything that is food tastes good. After being brought up with no food and having junkies for parents, you learn to appreciate food.

I watch Ky take a bite. I can tell he likes it because he goes for a second bite.

"Good?" I ask.

"Tell me, why don't you like Pizza Hut?" I freeze, placing the pizza back in the box. "The real reason this time."

He sips from the straw of his Coke, waiting for me to answer. I pick up the soda next to his, open it, place the straw inside, and do the same, buying me more time. I've never talked about it. It's not like anyone would care anyway. He's quiet, waiting for my response.

Another second turns into a minute.

I release a pent-up breath, placing the can of Coke near the box. "I told you already." Giving him a vague answer.

"You told me a lie, and now, I want the truth, Rubi." He shrugs. "What's the worst that could happen?"

He's right. It's not like he would care or do anything about it. It was a long time ago, but some memories don't go away. They come back like pulling the trigger and the gun going off.

"How do you know I was lying?"

"Because you were raised by animals. Animals that forgot to

feed the young. When the young are hungry, they aren't picky about their food. I'm sure if there was a box of Pizza Hut, you would have eaten it."

Ky is not only dangerous, but he's also smart. Really smart —— perceptive.

I swallow thickly and tell him the truth. "My stepfather had a friend named Mike. He was always at the house when my stepfather would come home. He would offer to buy me Pizza Hut because he knew I was hungry."

I pick up the pizza and take another bite, hoping he won't push for more, but his jaw is set. I can feel his gaze on me, waiting for me to swallow the food in my mouth, but I can't see his eyes behind the dark lenses of his sunglasses.

"What did he want?"

I place the pizza back in the box, wiping my hands with a napkin, knowing I only have about fifteen minutes left until the bell rings.

But I tell him.

"He would look at me funny. He would wait until my parents were high until they passed out. He knew my mother would never make me dinner, breakfast, or lunch. She would sell the food stamps for drugs. Until one day, he started telling me to call him daddy Mike. He said if I would sit on his lap, he would buy me Pizza Hut. I could never forget the look in his eyes when he said it. His eyes were big, like saucers, like they get when you're on that stuff. He would rub his hand over the bulge in his pants while he said it and lick his lips. I knew what he wanted and what it meant. I was afraid of him. He was bigger than me. I ran to my room and crawled out my bedroom window because it grossed me out, and I was scared. I hated Pizza Hut after that——" I glance at him—— "I love pizza. I love food. The kind I've had the privilege to eat and the kind I hoped to try if I got the chance. Just not that kind. Pizza Hut reminds me of daddy Mike."

My stomach turns, but not from hunger.

I get up suddenly, losing my appetite and thinking about the past. "I gotta get back to class. Thanks for the food, by the way." I make it to the last bleacher and jump off, blinking back the sting of tears.

"Rubi?" I turn around and look up. "You're right, Pizza Hut sucks. The New York style is way better."

CHAPTER THREE
Ky

AFTER FOLLOWING TYLER WITH RUBI, making sure she made it home safely after school. I go home and change, thinking about what Rubi said, hating something trivial. One would think it's stupid, but deep down, I knew better, not as a kid, but when I was older, and my memories of our conversations would replay in my head. Whoever would hear it coming from her would think she is a spoiled brat.

I drive to the other side of town where Cesar and the crew are living in the house my father set up as a fusion center to deal drugs. I usually go with Chris and Tyler, but this is about Rubi, and when it comes to her, I don't trust them.

I park my BMW in the driveway, and the house is full of gang members hanging outside on the wrap-around porch, drinking and smoking. Girls are sitting on their laps, hoping to get lucky. You could see the color of their thongs through their thin skirts and dresses despite the coolness of the night.

Almost every night, there is a party here. Not because that is all Cesar and his crew do, but it's a way that he can move merchandise and sell locally. That is how he makes his money, and I get my cut. I'm not proud or need the money, but if it's not me, then it's some prick my father would hire and skim off the top running a muck. My father wouldn't care as long as he moved product.

"What's up?" Cesar greets me as soon as he spots me inside.

"I need to talk to you."

He slides his arm away from the chick on his lap. He taps her on the thigh, signaling for her to get up. She gives me a once over, liking what she sees. Normally, I would take someone like her by the hand, push her into the next room, and take her against the wall. But that was before, and this is now.

Cesar follows me to the back room. He closes the door behind him, and I sit behind the desk. "I need to pay a visit to someone, and I need you to go with me."

It was easy to find the person I was looking for, especially since they hung out close by.

He nods. "Okay, when?"

"Now."

He crosses his arms over his chest. "How many of us do you need with you?"

I stare at his pretty boy face. "Just you."

I'm still deciding on what to do with Cesar. I keep convincing myself to let him live, but then that ugly feeling sprouts in my gut, imagining him with her. Jealousy is a bitch. It flares up like a rash. I bite the side of my tongue, the metallic taste of copper filling my mouth to keep me from killing him right here in this room.

"What car are we taking?" He asks.

"The black Charger."

He wants to know why and where, but he knows not to ask. I call the shots. What I say goes. No questions. No answers. Unless I want them.

I walk into the hallway, and the same girl saunters up to me and places her finger on the collar of my shirt. I look down at her finger and then up to her face. She's pretty with dark hair and dark eyes but not my type. To fuck, maybe, but not the kind I like touching me like she has a right to. There is only one that does, and she is not her. I peel her finger off the collar of my shirt.

Cesar walks up and grabs her by the waist. "Come on, he's not for you."

"You're for me," she says with a smile, looking directly at me. I blink. "How about I take care of both of you," she offers with a salacious smile.

"Only a weak man accepts desperation. A girl willing to take anything offered shows the true nature of her character."

She pulls back, looking insulted. "What does that mean?"

"It means you can't be trusted. I can tell you want to suck all the cocks inside this house, and you would do it. Just so you can feel special, but, in the end, you'll just be used. Do you like to be used?"

"You're crazy."

I lean close. "But you're willing to let me fuck you, and you don't even know my name or if I'll kill you when I'm done because you like the brand of my t-shirt." I lean back, hating the smell of her perfume. "But I'm crazy." I look at Cesar. "Throw her out."

When I walk out of the house rubbing my shirt where she had her fingers like it's dirty. Who knows how many cocks she's touched before I arrived.

"Damn, Ky. You good?" Cesar says, walking up to the driver's side of the black Charger after he told her to leave and not come back.

"Don't have girls like that up in the house. Too much of a liability. She'll rat you out or fuck the enemy. She didn't know who I was, and she was offering to give me whatever I wanted."

"I'm never one to turn down free pussy these days, but I get it. You call the shots." He chuckles, shaking his head. "But it's funny."

We both slide in the car and shut the door. "What is so funny?"

He fires up the car, "You are nothing like your father."

"I take that as a compliment."

My father would have grabbed her by the neck, bent her over the nearest table, and fucked her while everyone watched. Then, he would have thrown her out.

I give him the address, and he inputs it into the GPS. Twenty blocks later, we pull up to a house that looks abandoned, but in this neighborhood, we know better. There is no such thing as an abandoned house with drug addicts lurking around.

"What's here?" He asks.

"Daddy Mike."

I check my app on a burner phone, and right on cue, I see the delivery driver with the little pizza sign above his Hyundai approaching with the little red hat symbol.

I open the door and wave the guy over. He hands me the pizza, and I tap the car's roof, telling Cesar to get out. "Let's go."

"What does Daddy Mike and Pizza Hut have to do with why we are here?" Cesar asks.

I shut the door. "So there's this girl––"

"You're talking about Rubi." A slow smile creeps up my face, glancing at Cesar. "What does being here have anything to do with her, but more importantly, why her Ky?"

"Because no one like her exists." I nudge my head toward the house. "You'll understand why we are here in a minute."

We walk up the cracked concrete pathway between the two patches of dirt on each side, where there was once green grass leading to the single wood door. The door looks like it has been kicked in several times. The place is a shit hole, and it doesn't look better as the sun sets and the night sky sets in. The windows are boarded up, which serves my purpose.

"Cover the peephole," I tell Cesar. I bang on the door. Thump. Thump. "Pizza Delivery!" I shout. I hear movement behind the door.

After a minute, I hear the lock turn. The door swings open, and I kick it in, hearing a loud bang as it hits the asshole who opened it on the head.

"What the fuck! We didn't order no pizza."

I grimace when the stench of meth and body odor hits me. I can hear Cesar cough beside me as he struggles with the smell.

My eyes scan the living room, and there are broken bottles and drug paraphernalia strewn across the dirty carpet. A woman is smoking a glass pipe with a spoon in her hand, sitting on a green sofa with holes and dark stains.

I turn to the man, pressing the palm of his hand over his busted forehead. Blood is spilling down his face.

"Where's Mike?"

"I don't know who the fuck you're talking about." I kick his knee, and he falls to the ground on his back. Cesar draws his gun and points to his face. "Come on, man! I didn't do anything."

"Wrong answer," I grit. "Let's try again. Where's Mike?"

His face contorts and points to the back hallway. "First door on the left."

"How many men are in the house?" I ask.

"Four, including me."

I look at Cesar. "What do you have on you?"

He knows I mean drugs. Drugs he would sell anyway.

"Molly, meth, coke, heroin and weed."

"Give me the meth."

He digs in his pocket and hands me the small bag of crystal meth.

I take it and hold it out to the drug addict on the floor. The woman on the couch turns her head, her eyes widening like she just saw Jesus walk the earth.

"If you four assholes do what I say, you guys get to party."

The woman gets up and stumbles over. "I'll do whatever you want, baby."

Her blonde hair is matted to her head like she hasn't washed it in months. Her skirt is hanging off her bony hips. She is all skin and bones, and when she talks, you can see she has only three front teeth and one left at the bottom.

Meth. It smells like death, and it kills you slowly. Too bad for Mike. It won't be that easy.

"Make sure no one comes through that front door until we leave," I tell her.

She holds up her skinny hands and smiles. "Sure thing." She pops her lips, and I almost throw up. "I'll suck your dick if you want."

"Nah, sweetheart. I'm not here for that. You keep an eye on that front door, and I'll give you your candy."

She walks over to the front door and almost trips over the

man on the floor. She kicks him with her dirty heel. "Move the fuck out of the way, Hank. We got company."

Cesar snorts, and I glance at him with a smirk. "Let's go."

We make it to the door of the room where Mike is supposed to be, and without knocking, I kick it open.

Three men are sitting on an old mattress on the floor, passing a glass pipe, trying to get the last of whatever they had, their eyes looking at us in surprise. They look like mechanics. Jeans full of dirt and oil. A dirty, threadbare white tank top on each of their bodies. Dirt on their necks glistening with sweat and red eyes.

"Mike."

The one with the mullet hair turns his head.

Bingo!

His face is sunken and full of scabs. His arms have dark spots like he's been picking at his skin.

"How did you get in here?" Mike asks.

I hold up the bag of crystal meth, and they all look at me like I'm a God.

"Now that I have your attention"–– I glance at Cesar–– "hold him down."

Cesar walks over and grips Mike by his greasy hair, pushing his face into the pissed-stained mattress with the gun aimed at his temple. "Don't move."

"What the fuck, man! I didn't do anything!" He bellows.

The other two hold their hands up, looking between Cesar and Me.

"You want this?" I dangle the bag in my hand. They both nod. "Good. Do as I say, and you all get to party with your friends."

They both nod in tandem. "W-what do you want?" The one closest to Mike asks.

"You'll see."

I walk over with the pizza box, placing it on the bed beside Mike. "Do you remember... say... eight or nine years ago? A little girl with strawberry blonde hair?"

Cesar draws his brows together in confusion but then presses

26

the tip of the gun to the back of his head. "Answer him!" He yells in anger.

He sees where I'm going with this and why I brought him with me--alone.

"N-no. I don't know who the fuck you are talking about," he spits.

I nod in annoyance, knowing he is lying. "Hmm...let me refresh your memory. You would ask her to call you daddy Mike." He closes his eyes, and I continue, "You asked her to sit on your lap with your hard, pathetic, meth-infested cock in your pants and told her you would buy her pizza from Pizza Hut if she did." He remains still without another word.

I nod at Cesar. He lifts the gun and hits him with it on the back of his head. "Come on, Man!" He cries in pain.

I clench my teeth. "Answer me! Do. You. Remember."

"Yes! Alright. Yes. Her name was Rubi or something. They sold her to me. Her parents told me I had to get her to agree for me to touch her. I couldn't force her because of the cops at school finding out. That is all I know."

I can feel the bile rising in the back of my throat. Motherfuckers. I also know that an addict would do anything for the next hit. Human trafficking, stealing, or selling whatever they can get their hands on of value. Anything someone else would want if it means they get the next hit.

I look at the pizza. The cheese that looks like this fucker's face hating the smell...hated myself for making Tyler order it that day in his house. Rubi's voice in my head on repeat. I hate Pizza Hut. The New York kind is better.

"Me, too," I say absentmindedly.

"What?" Mike asks nervously.

I look over at the two meth heads leaning with their backs against the wall, their eyes trained on the bag inside my front pocket like dogs that would do anything for a treat.

I point my finger to Mike's backside. "Pull his pants down and take turns."

I pull the bag of meth out of my pocket and shake the bag.

They both go for the buttons of their jeans like they need to piss. I turn my head, looking away, hearing the onomatopoeic sound of zippers.

Mike begins to scream. "No! You bastards!" He squirms. I grab a slice of pizza and stuff it in his mouth while the guys do their thing, muffling his screams.

He tries to kick his legs, but Cesar snarls, pressing the gun to his head. "Move, and I'll blow you're fucking head off, *Cabron*."

He tries to scream, spitting the pizza out of his mouth, but I keep stuffing his face with another slice. "Who's your daddy now!" Huh!" I turn my face, looking at the second guy. "Fuck him harder, or you don't get shit."

He nods and goes at it. I block each sound of his pathetic grunts. I don't think about the fucked-up shit I'm allowing to happen. I think about Rubi and what this bastard said repeatedly. What he almost did. How scared she must have felt. I think about the system and how it fails kids like her.

When the second guy is done, I nod to him. "You got a needle? Spoon and a light."

He nods, "Yeah."

"Get it."

My eyes dart to Cesar and he nods in understanding, handing me the heroin blocking out Mike crying in pain from his bloody ass.

When I'm done, Mike's eyes look lifeless, with vomit all over the bed.

Cesar and I walk out of the room. I toss the bag of meth to Hank. The other two addicts walk around from behind us after they pull their pants up. "Not a word to anyone, or I'll come back, and you'll end up like Mike."

"Not a word," Hank says, practically salivating, holding the bag of meth in his hands and walking over to the couch.

We head out and get in the car. "You got a clean T-shirt?" I ask. "I smell like shit."

I need a shower.

Cesar glances at me before he pulls out onto the road. "I was about to blow that fucker's head off."

"I know, but I needed it to look like an overdose."

"How did you know?"

This was the part I was dreading. The twenty fucking questions.

Deflecting the question, I reply, "I know things, Cesar."

"But how did you know? I've known Rubi way before you."

"Let me ask you a question, Cesar. Did you fuck, Rubi?" I ask changing the subject.

I grind my teeth because I know he's had sex with Rubi. He was her first, but I need to hear it from him. I need to see if he has the balls to tell me. He grips the steering wheel, glancing between me and the road. Until finally...

"Yeah," he says quietly.

So he has balls.

"Touch her again, and I'll kill you."

"It wasn't like that--"

"You heard me. Touch her again, and I will kill you."

I hear him let out a pent-up breath. He knows not to question me or why I feel the need to unalive him for touching her. I run shit. Not him. Not even my father. Not regarding her.

"Yeah, I heard you."

"Good, I'm glad we understand each other."

The air in the car turns thick with tension for the next five minutes. Cesar is staring straight ahead out the windshield. The silence begins to stretch. Then, I shove him lightly on his shoulder and give him a malevolent smile. I watch his throat swallow convulsively, his knuckles white, gripping the steering wheel. He's nervous, so I try lightening the mood.

"What's up with you and that girl wanting to fuck every guy that walks in the house? The one I saw on your lap. You know there are better girls that hang out at the house."

He shrugs. "That girl was easy. You know I hate it when they get clingy. With girls like that, you slap two condoms, and you're good."

I lean back in the seat, shaking my head. "Whatever you say, man."

"I love her." My head whips in his direction, surprised he has the balls to admit he has feelings for her. "Rubi... I mean... I love her, but I know I'm not good enough for her. I never was. I just... it was never supposed to happen... her and me. I was trying to get her to forget what almost happened." *Yeah, with your cock.* "She wasn't in a good place." I can find plenty of ways that he could have made her forget, and a cock isn't what I come up with.

He tells me the same story she did that day in the storage closet at school. Guilt claws at me for how I have treated her. It wasn't her fault, and it wasn't his. But I'm jealous he had her first. In a perfect world, she was supposed to be mine, and I was supposed to be hers.

He didn't know.

It's probably the only reason he is still breathing. He saved her when I wasn't around, and I have to respect him for that.

When he's done, I ask, "Where is the fucker that did it?"

He sighs. "I'll get you the info." He pulls into the driveway next to my BMW. "I don't want to overstep, but why are you doing all this?"

My eyes meet his, telling him the truth. "Because no one did."

CHAPTER FOUR
RUBI

"ARE YOU STILL MAD AT ME?" Tyler closes the driver's side door and starts his truck. "You can't keep giving me the silent treatment."

I have no right to be mad. He did nothing for me to be giving him the silent treatment, but I'm pissed for Abby.

I check my phone for the millionth time. Nothing. No text from Ky. Maybe I'm getting way over my head, hoping he'd change.

"I'm mad at you. That's what people do when they are mad at people and don't want to deal with the issue, so they don't talk about it."

"So pretending the reason doesn't exist and giving the other person the silent treatment is the answer. Expecting it to blow over like it didn't happen. But the thing is, Rubi. Nothing happened. I messed around with Amber. Last time I checked, I don't have a girlfriend."

He's right. He technically doesn't.

"Did you sleep with her?"

It's none of my business, but I keep telling myself I need to know because it would help me deal with Abby and her feelings. She's a junior, and Tyler is going off to college as planned, but when you like someone, you don't think about the bigger picture. You think of the moment, and feelings get magnified.

He glances at me briefly. "You really want to know?"

"Yes, just in case I run into Amber at the house."

He snorts. "That would never happen. I would never bring her over to the house out of respect."

"For what?"

"You, Rubi. I would never do that to you. She wasn't part of what happened on your birthday, but she was there, and she knows that Jen and her friends don't like you because of Ky. She swears she had nothing to do with it, but I'm not sure about her yet."

I roll my eyes because she probably knew, and she is team Jen. "Did you?"

He swipes his hand over his face. "Yeah, I did." I nod, running my tongue over the front of my teeth. Poor Abby. "Are you mad?"

I shake my head. "You're my half-brother. Why would I be mad, but you made a choice."

He scoffs. "What is that supposed to mean?"

"Nothing. You chose to sleep with Amber. The only problem I have is how she treats Abby, but Abby can put you in the same boat as Amber now."

Silence.

Then he surprises me by saying, "Abby and I are close friends because of Chris, and she's his little sister. She has no reason to be mad at me, but I understand. She probably thinks that I'm going to make fun of her like Amber did because of her dance routines at the games. They suck, and she does look disjointed when she dances, but she still has her whole senior year left. She's seventeen. Amber and Jen graduate this year. She'll be fine."

"Good to know. I'll have a little talk with her."

He parks in the senior's parking spot. "You would do that?"

"Sure. Why not? She's been nice to me since I got here. Like you said, there is nothing she should be mad about. Whatever is bothering her, she'll get over it. Don't take it personally if she ignores you for a while. Girls have a funny way of getting over things."

She will not get over it that easily, but I don't tell him that. It's obvious he doesn't like her in that way. She's his best friend's little sister, and I get it. Bro code and all that.

I wonder if Ky sees me the same way, but it wouldn't make sense because Ky doesn't care what anyone thinks. I woke up in the closet this morning, but I noticed the bear that Chris won me at the fair was missing.

I jump exiting Tyler's truck and spot Jen walking over with Amber.

"Hey, are we good for the movie tonight?" Amber asks, sliding her hands around Tyler's waist. He looks down at her with a tight smile. "Yeah, I'll pick you up at seven."

Jen's gaze slides over to me with an apologetic grin. "I'm sorry. Rubi. About the night at your birthday party. It was cruel, and I didn't know... It was supposed to be a joke."

"Funny."

She looks at Tyler. "I'll be at Ambers so you and Ky could pick us up and save the trip," Jen says to Tyler. My stomach dips.

I glance at Tyler for confirmation, but he's looking directly at Jen when he replies, "Yeah, we'll both be there."

I walk away, feeling my heart being split in half with a knife. Ky forgave her for what she did, like it was nothing. I would have expected that from Tyler. But from Ky?

But then the fair happened and the house of mirrors on the same night. How he made me feel. The way he pleasured me. My thoughts go to what I said to him yesterday at lunch. The way he bought me my favorite pizza and I opened up to him about my past, telling him something no one knew.

I was abused by meth addicts. He's probably disgusted with me imagining all the worst kinds of things. I should have never opened up to him and accepted the truth. Before I came here, Ky had a life without me.

"Hey." I look up to see Abby giving me a small smile.

"Hey," I chirp.

"Are you okay? Did someone say or do something?"

I open my bag and slide the Algebra 2 book I need inside my locker. "I'm good."

She bites her lip nervously, clutching her textbook to her chest. "Do you want to go with me and Noah to see a movie?"

"I don't think that's a good idea. Look what happened last time."

She looks at her feet. "Look, I really would like you to come. I don't care about what happened, and neither does Chris." I raise an eyebrow when she looks up. "I know about Tyler and Amber"--she swallows-- " and Jen. Chris mentioned it to me. It won't be at the same movie theatre. I convinced Noah to take me to another one across town."

Her reminding me of Ky taking Jen out is like ramming a nail inside a coffin.

"Won't I be a third wheel or something?"

Her eyes light up. "No, because Chris is going. He was kind of hoping you would agree."

I frown. "Why hasn't he asked me?"

"He's...afraid you'll turn him down," she admits.

"Why?"

"He was kind of embarrassed at the fair the other night because of Ky."

"I had a great time," I tell her.

Liar. Ky gave you a great time.

"I tried to tell him that, but he isn't convinced. And Ky acting like his crazy self doesn't help."

"I'm not worried about Ky. He's going with Jen, Tyler, and Amber to the movies."

"Is that... a yes?" She asks with a hopeful expression.

I nod. "Yeah. Count me in."

She smiles. "I'll tell Chris," she says in excitement. I close my locker. "And Rubi?" I look up. "Thank you."

I watch her turn with a smile, walking down the hall to her class. I have to admit, we both have something in common. We're both trying to get over someone.

I walk into Algebra 2 and sit, opening my textbook to the lesson Mrs. Keller has us working on. My eyes keep darting over to Ky's empty seat. I find Jen and Nicole whispering to each other, looking straight at me.

"Don't pay attention. They're just jealous of you." I turn my head in the opposite direction and catch Chris's gaze. He nods his head at them. "That's what girls do when they feel threatened by someone prettier than they are." A blush stains my cheeks.

I'm sure Abby already told him I said yes about tonight. "You think I'm pretty?" I ask.

"Hello to you, too," he teases. "But yeah, of course, I think you are pretty. Gorgeous, in fact."

I pinch my brows together. "You don't have to lie to me. You had me at pretty." I grin. "I'm still going with you and Abby to the movies."

But his expression turns serious. "Why would you think I would lie about something like that?"

Because I look like a monster. I can't even wear a backless dress or top. There is nothing gorgeous about that. Jen and Nicole are stuck-up bitches, but they are beautiful. They don't have ugly scars.

Ky's words burn in the back of my mind. The girls I fuck around with are more my style. Clean, pretty, and have something going for them.

I lick my lips. "It's no secret, but I think you know why."

I'm saved from answering by the door opening, and Mrs. Keller walks in. Silence quickly blankets the room, and everyone shifts in their seats. Mrs. Keller greets everyone by writing on the dry-erase board and adding the current lesson at the bottom. I face forward but find my eyes darting to Ky's empty seat.

The sound of the door opens, and I look up to find Ky walking in late, handing Mrs. Keller a tardy pass. She looks at it and nods, indicating for him to take his seat.

He walks down the aisle. I could see from the corner of my eye he was looking at Jen and Nicole. He took the empty seat before me, and I could smell the scent of his ocean-scented body wash, fresh from a shower. I slide my notebook on my desk and turn to the page to start working on the lesson.

The rest of class time moves in silence.

He doesn't turn around.

He doesn't look at me.

He hasn't texted me. The biggest blow is when he smiles at Jen and Nicole. It's obvious he is done messing with me.

But I make sure I don't fall for his shit a third time. I open his contact on my phone before the bell rings and block his number. I also make a note to lock the bedroom window when I get home.

When I was eleven, he was all I could think about. I even have the scars to prove it. When I was taken away, I had to learn to live without him. But let's face it: it's difficult to let go of the person you care about the most. But now that I've found him, it's even harder to hold on to the memory of a person who doesn't care about you in the way you hoped.

I have to learn to find peace.

I have to learn to let him go.

CHAPTER FIVE
RUBI

CHECKING the mirror one last time, I slide my thumb under my bottom lip line, wiping a bit of lip gloss. I'm wearing ripped jeans and my favorite Seether's T-shirt, two sizes too big, hanging off one shoulder I was able to find in the donation box at the group home. I walk over to the bedroom window to make sure it's locked and can't be opened from the outside, pushing it up with my hands. Satisfied there is no way Ky could come inside, I close the curtains and make sure Hope has food and water.

Knock. Knock.

"Rubiana? Abby is here."

I open the door and see my father, Stephen, sporting a lazy smile. I step out, closing the door behind me.

"Thank you. I promise to be back in time."

"Midnight," he says, reminding me I'm still on probation.

"Okay."

He nods, stepping back to let me pass. "Rubiana?" He calls out.

I turn. "Yeah."

He runs his fingers through his hair. "Chris is a good kid, but"––he walks and stopping before me ––"his father has plans for him." Meaning I'm not good enough.

I thought it was the other way around. A girl's father should say that about the guy she is going out on a date with because, no matter what, she's his daughter. Since I arrived, it has been a litany swirling in my head. Lurid and cruel. My father doesn't see me as anything other than a mistake.

41

Unworthy.

Pitiful.

"I understand. I never thought I was."

"What do you mean?"

"Good enough." I turn, walk down the stairs, and leave the front door where Abby is waiting, feeling hollow inside. There is a reason Stephen Murray brought me here. I don't know what that is yet, but it wasn't so he could get to know his daughter better or save her from foster care.

"Hi, I hope it was okay. Chris and Noah came in separate cars. I wasn't sure what time you had to be back and didn't want to risk it getting you back past curfew."

"Midnight, like Cinderella."

"Lucky. My dad said eleven thirty, but Chris doesn't have one. It's unfair, but it's because Chris told him we were going in two cars. My dad isn't sold on Noah yet."

I wish my father cared for me like that. My curfew is because I'm on probation. If it wasn't for that, I'm sure I wouldn't have one. I'm positive a drug dealer could take me out, and Stephen Murray wouldn't give a shit about it.

Chris gets out of his Maserati, and I can tell he's nervous. He keeps looking toward the front door like someone is going to run out and attack him. Don't worry, it's me they are worried about.

His eyes finally land on me with a smile, sliding his hands into the front pocket of his black jeans. "Are you ready?" He asks.

"Yeah." I look over at Abby. Noah is holding the passenger door open so she can get inside.

When I step forward, he walks over and does the same. "You look great, Rubi," he says when I'm about to slide inside the car, leaning in slightly and giving me a soft kiss on my cheek. My head turns, taking me by surprise, causing his lips to brush against mine. Shit. I pull away, embarrassed, and slide in the seat.

"I'm sorry," I say once he starts the car.

He glances at me with a smile. "There is nothing to be sorry about." He places the car in drive, waiting for Noah to pull out ahead. "I'm not."

I can still feel the tingle of his lips on mine. I rub my lips together, reminding myself that I applied lip gloss. It's still there, but not as much as before. My cheeks heat, wondering if some rubbed off on him. I close my eyes for a moment, feeling awkward. It was an accident. I shouldn't feel guilty. Ky is on a date with Jen.

"We don't have to watch the same movie."

I glance at him. "Okay."

He took the same effort as the other night at the fair. He is wearing a different cologne, though. This one smells like citrus.

"You smell nice." He glances anxiously at me for a split second but says nothing. "Your cologne.... it smells good."

"It's new," he replies.

I'm not good at socializing. There were only two people on the planet that I talked to about personal things. Now, I have no one. Cesar is on the other side of town doing his *thing*. Ky has turned out to be someone I don't trust. I have no friends except Abby, and we are not that close. Tyler doesn't count because I would never tell him anything personal.

Chris pulls out his phone and connects it to the car's Bluetooth. I smile when Seether's Broken starts playing.

"You like Seether?" I ask with a grin.

"I do, but who doesn't."

"You'd be surprised." Kids in the group home would give me shit when I played it.

I'm relieved when Chris offered to watch a slasher flick. Abby wanted to watch a romance movie, which was the last thing I wanted to watch. The only downside was when the guy with the mask found the girl hiding in the closet with a butcher knife. I jolt when he pulls the closet door open, causing me to turn my face and prompting Chris to pull me close to his hard chest. It was innocent, like the brush on my lips. It's what I keep telling myself. But I know to Chris, it isn't. I don't know if that is a good thing or a bad one. But he's here trying to show me a good time. It's better to be around someone that wants you than to be around someone that doesn't.

Chris laces his fingers with mine when the movie ends, and we walk toward the parking lot to his car. Abby and Noah are still inside. Their movie ends in ten minutes, but I still have time until I need to head back home.

"Are you hungry? He asks. "We can––"

I gasp, blinking three times to make sure I'm not hallucinating.

Chris releases my hand, placing both of his hands on his head. "Fuck!"

I take a ragged breath, watching in horror. Chris's Maserati is all busted up. The windows, headlights, taillights, and all four tires are slashed. The entire car is keyed with the letters PUSSY carved on the side, including the hood.

"Who would do this?" I ask.

He shakes his head, walking around the car and inspecting all the damage. He looks up, and I can see the anguish in his eyes. "I don't know."

My thoughts automatically go to Ky, but he's in the theater on the other side of school with Tyler and Jen. There is no way he can be at both places simultaneously, and Chris is one of his best friends. He wouldn't do this to him. Plus, Ky doesn't know I'm out with Chris and Abby.

"Do you, Tyler, or Ky know anyone that would do this, or maybe you pissed someone off. Or it could be someone that hates people with really nice cars and are shitty ass losers. We are closer to the other side of town. I don't want to be the bearer of bad news, but your car stands out in the parking lot," I say, rushing the last part out.

Abby and Noah walk out to the parking lot when their movie ends after Chris calls for a tow truck with wide eyes.

"Who the hell did you piss off?" Noah asks with a grimace.

"Holy shit," Abby says with a hand covering her mouth in disbelief.

Chris leans back on his car, scrolling through his phone, and begins texting. The light from the screen casts a glow on his face with a solemn expression.

"Could you take the girls home, Noah? Rubi needs to be home before midnight, and I need to be here when the tow truck comes."

"Of course, man. You want me to come back." He offers.

"Are you sure?" I ask Chris before he responds. I hate to leave him alone.

"How about we take Rubi home, and I'll come back with Dad?" Abby adds.

"No. I'll take care of it," Chris says. He looks up from his phone, and his eyes soften when they meet mine. "I'm sorry, Rubi."

Noah walks Abby to his car. Instead of following them, I walk up to Chris, rise on my toes, and give him a soft peck on the corner of his mouth. He closes his eyes for a second. "I had a good time tonight, and I'm sorry about your car," I say softly.

I land on my heels. He opens his eyes, sliding a strand of hair behind my ear. "I wish I could take you home. I keep skipping that part."

"Then say goodbye right here."

He pushes off his car, and I think he's going to kiss me. His eyes darken. My stomach clenches. I don't feel the magic feeling you hear about. I don't feel like time has stopped or excitement.

But I want to.

I feel his heat and scent of his cologne. Right when he leans in, his phone goes off and just like that, the moment goes up in smoke.

He pulls back and answers. "Yeah, in the parking lot by the movie theatre," he says on the phone. It must be the tow truck company.

Noah's car pulls up, and I silently wave before getting in the back seat. My phone buzzes in my pocket; I pull it out and see a text from an unknown number.

Unknown: Where are you?

I know it's Ky. He must have figured out I blocked him.

"That has to suck. I hope they catch the people responsible," Noah says.

"I feel bad for Chris," I add.

"He loves that car. He begged my parents for two years, convincing them to get it."

What's weird is that he didn't call the cops. I wanted to ask why he didn't, but I'm not sure Abby knows the answer. Things are not making sense. Ky's erratic behavior. Stephen warning me off Chris. Chris's car being vandalized. Everywhere I go, bad things happen. I expected that in foster care or back home, but not here.

CHAPTER SIX
RUBI

WHEN I GOT HOME last night, I shut off my phone, showered, fed Hope, and pushed the chest of drawers in front of the bedroom window. If Ky sneaks in, him moving it out of the way would wake me.

I could have simply told Stephen to arm the alarm, but then I would have had to explain why and what he said about me going out with Chris; any notion of him redeeming himself as my father vanished.

I walk in English, ignoring Ky, Tyler, Chris, Patrick, Jen, Tyler, and Amber, making my way to my seat when Ky walks behind me, his breath fanning my neck.

I didn't stop at my locker this morning, and I skipped the cafeteria for the football field at lunch. I wanted to be alone to gather my thoughts and come up with a plan. A plan to leave this town. Possibly Georgia, where no one knows me or my past. I could make up a story about where I grew up. Get a job and rent out a small apartment. I don't think about college because I have no way of paying for it, and even if I secured a scholarship, I wouldn't be able to support myself.

"Ignoring me isn't going to keep me away from you, Rubi. Nothing can," he whispers.

Good luck.

I take my seat, ignoring him. One thing I have mastered my whole life is ignoring people and keeping to myself.

The teacher, Mrs. Thompson, lumbers in the classroom, and I immediately pull out my writing journal. We are supposed to write a poem or a diary entry about our day, or how we feel, and when our name is called, we read them aloud. I already wrote mine, having nothing better to do in my room.

I sit and wait until my name is called, looking down at the words on a simple sheet of paper.

Lost in my thoughts. I hear my name being called. "Rubiana?" I look up at Mrs. Thompson. "It's your turn."

I nod, getting up, hearing whispers and giggles from Jen and Amber. But I don't care what they think. They can all have each other.

I hold the paper and begin.I found strength in being alone.

I found strength in being alone.
It is my superpower.
No one could take my love.
No one could take my breath.
No one could take my warmth.
No one could ruin my dreams.
Dreams of being kissed under the warm sun surrounded by daisies.
Taking my breath away.
Being loved.
But those are just dreams because dreams are not real.
Pain is real.
Especially when it's in your heart and the memory of it on your skin.
Because you wanted love.
To be wanted
To be held
To be the one they chose.

50

But it's all a lie because I'm still alone.

You can hear a pin drop inside the classroom when I take my seat and close my journal, slipping it inside my bag.

"Wow, Rubiana. Have you ever considered going to college for creative writing?"

I look up. "Huh?"

Mrs. Thompson raises her brows. "College?"

I shake my head. "I'm sorry. I-I'm not going to college."

She crosses her arms over her chest. "How come? You have the grade point average--"

"Girls like me don't get into college, Mrs. Thompson."

"It doesn't have to be that way, Rubiana. You have a talent for someone your age."

"I know different," I shoot back. "Where I come from, those are just dreams. I'm sure you read how I spend my summers." I watch her swallow and look away at her desk for a moment. I assumed right.

I figured Mrs. Keller would tell the teachers what I wrote on the first day of class. Mrs. Thompson remembered because I'm sure it was different than what anyone else in class wrote. That is what teachers do when they feel pity for students and read something that makes them feel empathetic. I got used to it when I was younger when teachers would ask what I got for Christmas.

The teachers would look at my shoes that were glued together and so dirty that I wondered how they got that way.

But it wasn't because I jumped in puddles or ran through the dirt every chance I got. I lived in a house with two meth addicts. They didn't take me back to school shopping.

Drugs were a norm in my neighborhood. There were more users than sellers. But I quickly figured out what the shoes tossed over the powerlines meant. Every street that drug dealers and users lived on had shoes tied by the laces thrown over the powerlines.

51

One day, it was raining, lightning struck, knocking a powerline, and the shoes fell on the sidewalk. They were two sizes too small, but I learned to deal with it. The ones I had, the sole finally detached that day, and my socks were peeking out. It was my tenth birthday on my way home from school. Some people might find that story sad or disgusting that I wore shoes that fell from a powerline, but it was my birthday present.

Ky turns around in his seat, and I feel the heat of his stare. But I keep looking at the burn mark on my hand. The one my mother gave me because I cried when I was hungry. The hunger pains got worse when I came home from school. I would get so hungry but I knew there was no food. I hoped my mother would see how much I was hurting and would give me something to eat. But I learned after that day that if you didn't eat, the hunger pangs would come in full force. Eventually they go away but that day, it hurt. If I stayed silent, it hurt. If I cried, it hurt, but then crying turned into burns that came with pain. So I stopped crying.

"How'd you get that?" Ky asks.

I don't answer, but from the corner of my eye, I can see Chris look over with a glare.

Ky's finger hovers over the burn mark from the meth pipe but I snatch it away, placing my hand on my lap under the table.

"Ky, do you want to volunteer and read yours?" Mrs. Thompson asks.

His eyes are black and dangerous but he doesn't turn around

"How'd you get that?" He repeats.

"Mr. Reeves." Mrs. Thompson calls out impatiently.

"I'm waiting," he says, not caring that everyone is now looking at us.

"Ky," Tyler calls out, trying to get his attention, but nothing. He doesn't flinch.

The muscle in his jaw tics. "How Rubi? Who burned you?"

Tears well up in my eyes. I do not want to answer him in front of everyone. I don't want to tell him anything else, but If I don't, he will make things worse because that is what he has done lately--make shit worse.

"Leave her alone, Ky," Chris warns.

"Mr. Reeves, you have disrupted the class long enough. I will have to ask you to leave or call security."

Nothing.

He continues to stare at me with his handsome face. "Answer me, *Corazon*."

"Don't call me that," I snap.

"You are."

I glance at Jen, her mouth turning into a frown and then at him. "Stop playing games."

"Answer the question, and I'll leave you alone... for now."

I let out a frustrated breath, ignoring Mrs. Thompson.

"I'm calling security--"

I sigh, trying not to blink to keep the tears at bay. "My mother." His eyes turn cold. "She burned me with a meth pipe on my tenth birthday so I would stop crying because I was hungry," I answer, my voice breaking on the last part.

The bell rings. I get up, grab my bag, and run out of the classroom.

"Rubi!" I hear Chris call after me over the horde of bodies flooding the hallway. I keep walking, but he runs after me. I turn around. "What?"

His eyes roam over my face, out of breath. "Is that true?"

I hate being mean to him, but I'm angry and embarrassed.

"Does it matter?"

"He shouldn't have pressed you like that. I'll deal with him."

"Don't bother." I move to turn away, but he grabs my hand. "I'm sorry, Rubi." I look up. His eyes are full of warmth. His thumb caressing the top of my hand. "I'm sorry she did that to you. I know it sounds stupid after all this time, but sometimes you need to hear it."

"Hear what?" Ky moves between me and Chris, causing him to drop my hand.

"Leave her alone, Ky," Chris warns, getting in his face.

"Or what?" Ky looks Chris up and down, sizing him up. "Do you think she needs your bullshit sympathy?" Chris's expression hardens when Ky points his finger an inch from his face. "Don't touch her."

Chris steps closer, their noses almost touching. "Or what?"

I look between them, worried that they will fight. I let out a relieved sigh when Tyler saunters up, breaking them apart. "What the fuck has gotten into you two? Are you serious right now?" Tyler looks at Ky. "Leave Rubi alone, Ky. What you did back there was fucked up. I told you to back off."

"That's not going to happen," Ky sneers.

"Why?" Tyler asks.

Ky smiles, but it doesn't reach his eyes. "Wouldn't you like to know?"

"Stop it. All of you." I walk up to them ignoring people walking by giving us curious stares. "I want to be left alone." All three glance at me in tandem. "I want to call a truce. I'll stay out of your way, and you stay out of mine." I shake my head. "I never wanted to come here in the first place, and when the school year ends, I'll leave."

"But you're here," Ky says.

"Unfortunately. Now leave me alone, "I reply, but his eyes hold mine in challenge, telling me I'm full of shit if I think it's that easy.

When I open my locker, a notebook paper is taped to the back of the door. I ignore the bell when it rings, taking the paper. A lump forms in my throat when I begin to read it.

> They're going to say I'm crazy, Rubi. That I'm obsessed with ruining you.
> But the truth is... they want to take what is mine.
>
> Ky

I slam the locker shut and ball up the paper in my fist. Ky is losing is damn mind or he is a psycho. Patrick warned me. He wasn't kidding.

I glance down the hallway, and it's empty. I pull out my phone and send a quick text to Cesar. He's the only one I could trust right now.

> Rubi: I need to talk to you in person.

I slide my phone in the pocket of my jacket. When I look up, I jolt.

Ky is leaning against the wall. He's more intimidating when standing this close, and no one is around.

"Where were you last night?" He asks like nothing happened in the classroom or hallway just minutes ago.

Is he for real?

"I went to the movies with Abby." It isn't a total lie. "Where were you?" I volley back.

His expression is murderous, and I get why no one messes with Ky. A nervous chill runs down my spine. I can feel my pulse racing in my veins. He smiles, easing his expression. "I went out with Tyler."

"I heard. On a date, along with Jen and Amber, to the movies.?" The smile wipes off his face. A classroom door opens, and he pulls me toward the back exit of the school.

I try to get away from his grip. "What are you doing? Let me go--"

"What does it look like? We're leaving."

My eyes widen in panic. "I can't skip school, Ky. I'm on probation."

He looks back at me. "You obviously don't know what I'm capable of."

"No, I don't." He tilts his head back and laughs like I said something funny. "You're crazy. This isn't funny."

"I never said it was, and for the record, I'm not crazy. I'm the sanest person you've met. Not to mention, I have bigger cojones."

"We'll, I wouldn't know. But I'm sure the cheer squad would."

He pauses, and I realize we are already in the student parking lot beside his car. He opens the front passenger door and leans close, his lips inches from my ear. "Get in." I want to tell him to fuck off. To scream. He must see the intent on my face. "Do it, and they will think you were skipping school. You're on probation, remember?"

My nostrils flare in anger. "Asshole," I mutter, getting in his black BMW.

He doesn't waste time firing up the car and cooling it down. It is still hot during the day, being mid-October–– two weeks until Halloween.

"Where you are taking me?"

He looks over. "My house."

I snort. "I thought I wasn't allowed to go there."

"You are always welcome there, but only when I'm there. I was mad at you before."

"Why?"

"Because you left me, and I didn't know why."

I wrap my hair, frustratingly twisting it up in a messy bun. "I was eleven, Ky."

"So. You weren't supposed to leave me."

"And what would you have done, huh?"

"I would have found you. You were never supposed to leave me, Rubi."

"Do you know how crazy you sound right now? I don't belong to you, Ky."

We are stopped at a red light, watching a couple cross the street on the crosswalk walk, holding hands. He turns to face me.

When I stare into his black eyes, it's like he has lived a thousand lives, and I'm in every one of them.

"You've always belonged to me, Rubi. Since the first day you jumped my fence when we were kids, you were mine."

"Then why did you go to the movies with Jen?"

There, I said it. Jealousy crawling over my skin, eating me alive.

"I didn't fuck Jen, and I didn't kiss her on the corner of her mouth either."

It was him! He vandalized Chris's car.

"It was you."

"Now you know. Don't ever go out with another guy that isn't me again. Don't block my number or shut your window. Block it with a dresser. None of that will keep me away from you, Rubi."

I pull him by the collar of his shirt, anger pulsing through my veins for making me feel this way, and pull him toward me, clenching my teeth. "Don't you ever... ghost me again. Now you know how it feels." We both stare at each other until the sound of a horn has me releasing the collar of his shirt.

"I know you're mad at me," he says as he continues to drive toward his house. "I have my reasons, Rubi, but you have to trust me. They all came from someplace good."

And that's the problem. I have a hard time trusting people. Even him.

CHAPTER SEVEN
RUBI

WHEN I WALK inside Ky's house, it still feels cold like the last time I was here and I can't shake off the feeling of sadness that washes over me. It feels like a place where everything bad happens when good surrounds it.

"Are you hungry?" He asks walking over to the sleek refrigerator. "*Tenemos, soda, leche y agua para tomar.*" I smile when he speaks Spanish. "Soda, milk and water. I also have some juice if you like. I can also make you a sandwich or order in anything you want." My stomach begins to growl and he raises a brow. "So, what will it be, princess?"

"I want Chinese food," I blurt.

I have never had Chinese food before. It can easily be ordered and hope it's not expensive. He pulls out his phone and begins to scroll closing the refrigerator. "If it's too expensive, it's okay," I rush out.

He looks up. "It's not. I got it. You don't have to worry about money when you're with me, okay." I nod. "What do you like?"

I bite my lip nervously and draw my brows close together. "I wouldn't know. I've never eaten Chinese food before."

"First timer," he says going back to his phone.

I wait, watching his thumb pressing on the screen for the next five minutes. When he's done, he opens the fridge and takes two sodas out. "Here, water is boring."

He walks toward the stairs handing me a soda can letting me walk ahead. "Where am I going?" I ask climbing the first couple of steps.

"To my room but I didn't want to waste the view." His hand slides up the back of my leg and I almost drop the can.

"Is that what you tell all the girls you bring here?"

I'm sure he's used that line plenty of times but he surprises me. When he says, "I wouldn't know. I don't invite girls to my room."

"What makes me so different?"

"You've let me in your room a bunch of times. It should only be fair, I let you in mine."

My cheeks heat but he isn't wrong. "You mean, you've let yourself in my room."

"Hey, you jumped my fence first. Fair is fair."

I laugh but it dyes off when he reaches the top of the stairs and stares at me. His eyes are hard like their possessed. The energy around us shifts like static electricity raising every nerve ending on my skin. It suddenly feels hot under my uniform jacket. I refuse to take it off because he would see the two letters of his name above the daisies tattooed on my skin.

He would know how much he means to me. How much he has always meant to me.

He steps forward and I can smell the scent of his rich spicy cologne. It feels like he is taking all the air and I'm struggling to breath. His eyes pin me to the spot. It so silent in the house, I can hear him breathing. He inches closer, his eyes never leaving mine.

"My room is this way, " he says walking down the hallway.

I close my eyes. *Get a grip, Rubi.*

I'm still standing by the stairs like an idiot looking around the sterile hallway when he walks in his room. With white walls and white floors. No picture frames.

I follow him inside and notice it is modern like the rest of the house. A modern queen bed in the center with end tables. The sheets are all white with gray pillows in the center. It looks inviting in contrast to the simplicity.

Instead of posters stuck on the walls like I'm used to seeing in most of the fosters homes I've been to, Ky's are framed. He has a poster of a black Lamborghini over his bed.

"Is that your dream car?" I ask remembering he wanted a car like Batman and it's not the BMW he drives.

He looks up at the framed poster of the cool looking car. "Something like that."

"The car you currently have is kind of similar in a way." I shrug opening the soda and taking a sip. "I mean, it isn't like Batman's but its close." I'm talking out of ass. I have no idea what these cars are worth and to be honest, I'm jealous that he drove his car with girls in the passenger seat when he always promised it would be me. It's stupid, but when you hold on to a promise for so long, you hope the other person doesn't break it.

He steps close causing me to walk back until the back of knees hits the edge of the bed. "Sit."

I do placing the soda on the floor careful I don't spill it.

He walks to his dresser giving me his back. I hear a drawer open and close. He returns with a dried-out daisy holding it out before taking a seat next to me. I look at the dried flower with faded yellow center with a single petal.

"Is this the one I left you?" He nods. "You kept it." I look down at the palm of his hand. "And the letter?"

"It's in my locker as a reminder."

"Of what?"

"That you left me." My chest squeezes tight because I didn't want to leave him. I would have never left. He nudges his head toward the flower in his hand. "You can have it back."

I remember playing *he loves me/he loves me not* with the daisies. There were only two times that the petal landed on *he loves me not*. The first, was the second time I visited Ky and went back home. My stepfather found out and he hit me. It was the day I received my first scar. The second, was the day I had to leave. The flower in my hand was a sign of how he would feel about me after I left and I didn't know it. I never wanted that. I wanted to be in his life but not like this.

"I never wanted to leave you... you know that right?"

He nods. "I know that now," he says quietly.

I close my hand on the flower feeling it crumble like it's the end of our childhood friendship. I guess it ended that day. I knew it was never meant to happen. A girl like me being friends with a boy like him. I didn't want to accept it and fought for it. For him.

"I guess we made promises to each other we could never keep, huh?" Our eyes meet. I see devastation in his pitch-black eyes. I sigh, looking out his bedroom window with a view of the backyard remembering our game. "Now I know why you burned it," I whisper.

"You promise to keep our treehouse?" I ask.

I like coming here. This treehouse feels like home. If I could stay here, I would. It makes me feel safe like I'm in a magical place not one can find me. But I know that is not true. My stepfather would find out and hit me again. Besides, Ky's parents will not let me take a shower here. I'm dirty and would probably dirty their pretty house.

"Yes, I promise," he says. "This is our treehouse. I would never get rid of it."

I smile. "Good," I say pleased, leaning on the wood slats. "Because I like our house."

He smiles grabbing more daisies so we can playing our game. We take turns asking a question and who whoever ends up with the last petal is there turn to answer. It is how we learned things from each other. Sometimes, I would silently ask if he loved me. No one had ever said the words before but I was hoping he would be the first.

"We were just kids. It was a stupid game. Time went by and every time I would look at it, it would remind me that you left without telling me why but I get it now. You had a valid reason. I was too stuck in my head to make sense of it."

My stomach sinks. It wasn't stupid. Not to me. But I'm not going to tell him that. He's over it––over me. Whatever we had as kids, the crushed-up daisy in my hand is proof of that.

"I never thought I would see you again." I blink back the sting of tears. "I'm glad I did though." I nod, struggling with my words. "Now we could move on from it."

He stares at me with a blank expression.

The doorbell rings. He takes out his phone getting up. "The food is here."

When we're downstairs, I look around for the trash to throw the dead flower but there is no sign of one. The kitchen looks empty with nothing on the counter. Every surface is wiped clean. There isn't a vase or a Keurig like in Tyler's house. I watch as Ky brings three bags full of food. The smell of food causes my stomach to groan like a monster lives inside me.

I watch as he opens the bag and takes out numerous white boxes and containers with Chinese symbols on them. My eyes widen at all the food wondering who else is coming over to eat.

"Who are all those for?"

He looks up. "For you mostly. You've never tried Chinese food before so I ordered everything. I thought you might like it with no vegetables. I remember you told me you didn't like vegetables."

I smile and my stomach does a little flip. "I still don't."

"I was right then. C'mere."

I walk over and see an empty bag and shake my hand inside disposing the dead flower. "Where's the soap and the trash."

He walks over and opens a cabinet door and pulls out everything I need to wash my hands. When I'm done, he's sitting on the other side of the island waiting for me. I look at all the neatly lined white boxes filled with different types of food. Rice, noodles, chicken, and beef in different sauces. There is even soup with dumplings inside them.

A little laugh escapes my throat when I look at all the food that smells delicious. "I've never seen so much food before."

He looks up and something shifts in his gaze, he swallows, and motions me over to the first box. I noticed he's removed his jacket and rolled up his school dress shirt revealing strong forearms. This close, I can see the tattoo on his left hand. There is a star and letters written in a language I can't pronounce. The letters are small but it's there.

He holds up a piece of beef on a plastic fork and blows on it to

63

make sure it's not too hot. "Here. Try this." I open my mouth and close my eyes in delight. It's full of flavor and the meat is soft. Salty, but just right. I open my eyes chewing on the piece of meat. "I think you might want to take your jacket off," he says softly. Chills snake up my arms when he unbuttons the first button, then the second. "You'll get it dirty."

I'm worried that he will see his name inked on my skin but I'm hot and he's right. I could get sauce on it. I let him slide the jacket over my shoulders and down my arms. My school dress shirt has short sleeves. His eyes trail the tattoos of the daisies over my arm. From this angle he can't see the two dark letters but when he lifts my arm to see the petals, he pauses. His eyes flick up to mine.

I bite my bottom lip nervously after I swallow the last piece of beef licking my bottom lip. I push my hair to the side away from the row of food on the island wanting the ground to open up and swallow me whole. "I guess now you know why I wear jackets and sweaters."

I remember hearing that it's bad luck to tattoo a guy's name on your skin. I didn't want to let go of Ky or our memories, but I guess they were right. It is bad luck. Especially when the guy hated you the whole time you were in love with him.

The air around us shifts. I don't know what to say. *I'll remove it when I get a job. I'll cover it up with a sharpie. I'll wear a band-aid until I can have it covered up.*

He clears his throat, glad when he moves to the next container not making a big deal out of it. This one has chicken with noodles. When I take a bite, I almost groan. "Oh my God. That is so good."

His eyes never leave my face while I'm chewing and doesn't move. I raise a brow. "What?"

He shakes his head with a grin. "Nothing. Do you want another bite or should we move on to the next one?"

I feel bad he hasn't had a bite to eat yet. "Which one do you like? You haven't eaten anything. Aren't you hungry?"

"I kinda like watching you eat." He admits. My tummy does a

little somersault and it's not because of the food. He takes another piece of chicken with noodles out of the container. When I open my mouth to take a bite, he waits until I have the chicken between my teeth and removes the fork.

I gasp when I'm about to chew, he takes the other side of the piece licking the dangling noodles from my chin. It's sexy. "It tastes better coming from you," he says against my mouth, taking a bite. He pulls away after there is nothing left.

"Thank you." He pinches his brows in confusion. "For the food," I add. "It's good. I can say I like Chinese food now. You have to tell me which dish is which though."

He grins. "You're welcome. I'll write all your favorite ones down for you but I'll remember them in case you forget."

I look around at all the containers that I haven't tried yet. "To be honest, I have a feeling I'm going to like them all. It's going to be hard to remember all of them."

"No it won't."

I angle my head to the side curiously. "How's that?"

"Because I remember everything about you, Rubi."

My heart races when he says things like that. It's scary. Possessive. I don't want to read too much into it but deep down I like it.

We spend the rest of the afternoon seated at the kitchen island sampling different types of Chinese food. I was right in liking most of what he ordered for me to try.

My phone rings and I know it is Tyler wondering why I'm not by his truck.

"I need to get home."

"It's not curfew yet."

"But Tyler--"

He holds a finger stopping me while he grabs his phone. His fingers fly across the screen and then he places it on the counter. "Done. I'll take you home when it's time."

"What did he say?"

His eyes lift. "To take you home. Now."

"What did you say?"

"That I will, but not right now."

"I don't want any trouble."

"You are not trouble, Rubi." He gets up from the bar stool. "They are."

I don't know what he means but I know he won't tell me.

Chapter Eight
RUBI

I SIT on the sofa in his living room and look at all the sleek furniture, noticing how different we were brought up. We come from different upbringings and how we clicked as kids. For me, it was easy; I had no one. But for him, he had everything. Maybe not a warm home, but he still had a home. Someone cared for him enough to give him the necessities. Luxuries. Things kids would die for.

He plops beside me instead on the sofa, our knees almost touching. My eyes are drawn to the tattoos on his hand. "What does the star mean?"

He places his hand on my lap and looks up at me. His gaze is warm, feeling like a caress over my face. "It means loyalty."

"To what?"

"Family," he says quietly.

"Your father?"

He nods. "And the fathers before him––" He turns his hand to the side where the words are written in another language inked on his skin––"*Lealta* is loyalty in Italian, and Mancini is my father's family."

"Why is your last name Reeves?"

"It's my mother's. I use it here for protection."

"Why? Are you in trouble? Is someone after you?"

He chuckles. "No, *principessa*."

"My father is Italian and my mother *was* Spanish."

He talks about her in the past tense, and my chest squeezes.

"She died?" He stiffens and nods.

69

"I'm sorry," I tell him, and I meant it.

"It's alright. She didn't care about me and left when I was little."

I can tell that messed him up. My mother messed me up, and my father didn't give a shit about me. He turned up a minute too late and three seconds short. My heart fills with guilt because he must have been angry and hurt when I left. No one wants to be abandoned by the people they care about. They want to be loved.

"I know I have said this already, but I'm sorry for leaving the way I did, Ky."

"It wasn't your fault."

"So, how did you get the name Ky?"

"My mother hated Italians," he deadpans.

I giggle, and he leans in, his lips a breath away. "How did she meet your father and have you then? How did you learn Spanish?"

"My father deals with a lot of different people from different countries. He thought it was best I learned. My father moved here because my mother was unhappy with his family."

"Where is he now?"

"Italy."

I raise my brows in surprise. Italy is far away. I'm surprised he leaves Ky here all by himself. He's eighteen, but still. He's all alone in this big house.

"Is he always gone?"

"Mostly. I have Tyler and Chris. We grew up together, after all. After my mother passed, he wanted me to leave with him to New York and travel abroad to and from Sicily, but I wanted to stay here. I was young. After my mother died, he didn't want to stress me out and decided to let me stay here in Georgia. He started the firm with Tyler and Chris's fathers after my mother left when she gave up on him—on us. I think it was her plan when she fell pregnant with me. It was easier to do it here where my father's family wouldn't interfere."

"That sucks."

"My father did everything for her, but it wasn't good enough. I wasn't good enough. She left anyway."

"What happened to her... after she left?" I croak.

"She died in an accident. She was pregnant with someone else's child on her way to see me after so many years. I think she hated my father for who he was, and therefore, she didn't want me."

"I wish I could say that a mother loves her child no matter what, but I'm not the right person to tell you that because I know that is bullshit. I've seen evil and stared into its eyes. It doesn't forgive. It takes, and it will destroy you if you think you can hang around and survive it. The worst part is when it's inside the person that created you, and there is nothing you can do." I look down at his hand on my lap. "You stop trusting people, KY."

"Do you trust me, Rubi?"

I swallow thickly because the truth is... I don't know. How can I trust him? How can I forget what he has done? He blows hot and cold. One second, he wants to humiliate and ruin me, and the next, I'm in his house, and he is buying me Chinese food and talking with me on the couch.

I'm so confused when it comes to him.

"I'll take that as a no," he says after five minutes of me going back and forth inside my head.

I pull back, creating some distance. "I don't know," I finally say. "Should I?"

"I'm the only person you could ever trust, Rubi. In time, you'll see. That is all I can tell you."

———

"I can't believe you skipped school and left with him?" Tyler scolds me when I get home. "He could have done anything to you and no one would have been able to help you. You know that, right?"

I throw my hands up frustratingly. "What is the big deal?"

Caroline and Stephen aren't home. They had to stay

71

overnight in New York for an important company function for building development.

"I'm in charge. I'm supposed to make sure you stay out of trouble. Ky is clever, Rubi. He knew that my parents wouldn't be home. If I didn't call him looking for you, who knows what he would have done."

"I think you're overreacting, Tyler. I thought Ky was your friend. Your...."

"He is, Rubi. But when it comes to you. He's.... unhinged for whatever reason."

Tyler looks away for a minute and then his head whips back in my direction. "Be honest with me. Have you had sex with Ky."

I think about the fair. The house of mirrors. Him eating me out. The rides with the vibrator he shoved up my pussy, going on ride after ride, and him turning it on, making me come without giving me a choice. We went on twenty-two rides like he promised and he made me come eight times, not including the house of mirrors. I haven't had traditional sex with Ky, so I go with a no.

"No. I have not had sex with Ky."

"Are you planning to?"

"That is none of your business. Why? Are you planning to have sex with anyone I should know about, and you feel guilty?"

"Don't." He walks behind me in the kitchen, where I'm making myself a cup of coffee, and grabs a mug to do the same. "Where did you go Tuesday night?"

"Movies with Abby."

"And...who else."

"Chris and Noah. Why?"

He loses his grip on the mug's handle and clanks on the counter. "Noah?"

"Yeah, Abby and Noah. She wanted me to go with Chris. I think Abby and Noah are getting serious." I hear the slam of the refrigerator door when he comes back with the creamer.

"Is she fucking him?"

I raise my brows and lean on the counter. "Why? Jealous? Is she not allowed to have sex with a guy her own age or something.

He likes her. She likes him. What's the problem? You fucked Amber, and God knows who else. Ky fucked Jen and probably half the school. I don't see the problem."

He scoffs. "You aren't wrong."

My insides bottom out because I know he is right. Ky doesn't have serious feelings for any girl. He burned our treehouse with all the daisies when he thought the worst of me. His mother left him and started another family without him. Of course he

"So, if me or Abby decide to screw someone, it's a big deal?"

He turns around with a glare. "You're my sister——"

"Half."

"Still, my sister and Abby... is my best friend's sister."

He can't be more obvious. Tyler has a thing for Abby. Interesting, but he won't do anything about it, or maybe wants to but feels guilty. The look on his face tells it all. He's jealous that Abby is going out with Noah.

Then I remember the look on Abby's face when she saw Tyler with Amber and he didn't care how she would feel about it. I hate him for pointing out about Ky having sex with all those girls at school. I want to get back at him. I want to hurt Tyler for making me feel so shitty.

"You know what, I hope she does."

"What are you talking about?"

"Abby." I stir the creamer in my coffee with a spoon. "I hope she finds happiness with Noah. If she plans to sleep with him or has already, good for her. It's not fair she has to watch you three assholes do whatever you guys want. Just because she is her brother's sister and a grade younger, she can't do shit. If it was me, I would have done it."

"Done what?" He asks with a hard edge to his voice.

"Had sex with a guy that treats me right. Maybe have a boyfriend. Girls have those, you know."

"Is that what you want? A boyfriend."

"I never said that."

"Then why are you leaving the school with Ky?"

He doesn't know our history, and I won't tell him. That is the only thing we have left between me and Ky. Our secrets. And his name is currently tattooed on my arm.

"Maybe he wanted to apologize."

He scoffs, "Yeah, by dragging you out of school to his house. He threatened anyone who would rat you out."

"How did he do that?"

Tyler rolls his eyes. "Ky can do a lot of things. That is what makes him dangerous."

"He is not dangerous."

Tyler crosses his arms and leans on the counter because we both know I'm full of shit. Ky is dangerous. But when I'm with him, I'm not scared he will hurt me physically, but my feelings are another matter.

"I don't think he is dangerous," I mutter.

"I don't want to see you hurt, Rubi. Ky"--he walks up to me--"is not a normal guy in high school. When you think he is your friend or boyfriend or whatever he makes girls think, he's like a switch, and he'll turn into a waking nightmare."

"Funny, I'm used to nightmares. I think I can handle it."

He closes his eyes because he thinks he is doing me a favor, warning me off Ky, but Tyler doesn't know the meaning of a nightmare. He hasn't had a hard day in his life.

He sighs. "Why don't you go out with a guy like Chris. You seem to like him. It's the second time you go out with him."

"It sucks what happened to his car. Did they catch the person who did it?" I ask, playing dumb.

He shakes his head but changes the subject. "What is up with you two?"

He means Chris and me.

"Nothing, we are just friends."

"Just friends?"

"Yeah, I don't think there is room in his life for someone like me."

"I don't get it."

"Ask your father. Apparently, I'm not good enough for your kind."

74

"My father said that?" He asks dubiously.

I pour out the rest of my coffee, not wanting to talk about it. "Something along those lines." I half shrug. "I'm used to it. It's no big deal."

"To what?"

I turn before walking out of the kitchen. "No one giving a shit about me. I know where I stand in all this, Tyler. I don't belong here."

CHAPTER NINE
RUBI

I SIT on my bed after feeding Hope, finding a place to move after graduation. How I plan to get there, and what options do I have in finding a job.

My phone vibrates on the nightstand. I unlock the screen and smile.

> Cesar: Miss me?

I smile. Thank God.

> Rubi: Took you long enough. Can I see you? Sperm donor is out with his wife. I need to talk to you. Where can we meet?

> Cesar: You'll violate probation, Rubi. If you get caught.

> Rubi: You'll make sure I won't.

> Cesar: Bad girl.

> Rubi: I never said I was a good girl. I'm bored. I need to talk to you.

> Cesar: Are you okay? Did someone touch you?

I think of Ky eating me out, and I squeeze my legs together.

> Rubi: Nothing like that.

I push the dresser and slide the window down enough so it's easy to get back inside. I grab my bag, taking my uniform in case I don't make it back in time and to get to school. Tyler left for Chris's house and said he would be back later so he wouldn't know I was gone.

I run down the sidewalk dressed in black and see the blacked-out Charger. I walk up, open the passenger door and slide in. Cesar's smell hits me with familiarity. Ocean-scented cologne and a hint of weed mixed with leather.

"Nice car."

"I got it six months ago."

He presses the gas, and the car roars down the street in the opposite direction.

"I missed you."

He turns his head. "Me too, *Nena*. I missed you, too."

"I need a favor."

"Name it."

"I need you to take me to a tattoo artist."

"More tattoos? I thought the sleeve on your right arm was all you needed."

"It is." I chew my lip nervously. "I need to cover up something."

He nods, and I'm relieved he doesn't push. "Alright. I know someone."

"I need it tonight. I also need to find a job away from here after graduation."

"Is that all?" He teases.

"I'm serious Cesar. I'm getting the hell out of here when I graduate."

"How about college?"

I snort. "Yeah, who's paying? You need money for college. What am I going to say to college admissions, huh? That my

78

mother was a meth addict, and I was taken away and sent to foster care. Where I would sneak out and steal food and clothes for the kids that didn't have shit and got caught." I blow out a puff of air and continue. "I'm on probation until I graduate and I'm broke. That's not something I should share with college admissions. I don't even have a license to drive a car, Cesar. You will tell me I deserve better, but I'll never get better."

"You have it good right now. You can make friends that have something going for themselves––"He swallows––"maybe meet someone that isn't a drug dealer and has something going for him. You're gorgeous, Rubi."

Tears sting my eyes because I know he is being supportive and understands we have been dealt a shitty life.

"I know you're supportive, but we both know I'm not gorgeous. You don't have to lie to me."

"I don't sleep with ugly girls."

I snort. "Do you know what they call me at school? Freak."

I tell him what happened on my birthday, and his jaw hardens. "I went on a date and that asshole that matches my DNA warned me off." I look out the dark-tinted window, watching the neighborhood change. The houses getting smaller. The cars getting older. "I thought it was the other way around, you know. I thought... fuck it."

I look over and Cesar is quiet. Like he's thinking. Then my stomach turns when he asks, "Is there any other person you want to talk about?"

"Huh?"

Then I remember the night when Ky got out of the car, and they had an exchange.

"You really know Ky?"

He nods. "I do." He looks at me after he places the car in park in front of a tattoo shop with a few guys smoking out front. "You need to be careful with Ky, Rubi."

"You're not the first. Tyler––my half-brother keeps warning me off."

79

"Because Ky isn't who you think he is. I don't think Tyler or anyone in West Lake does."

"But you do?"

"I do, and I cannot tell you because that would put us both in danger. Don't provoke him."

I know not to, but I want to know what Cesar thinks. I want to know his take on Ky from his perspective. Cesar isn't someone to mess with, and if he said stay away, I have to take his word for it.

"He provokes me."

Cesar closes his eyes and leans his head back against the head-rest. "Don't mess with him, Rubi."

"Why is he so dangerous?"

"Because he's obsessed."

"With what?"

"You, Rubi. He's obsessed with you."

I release a breath full of terror because I know he's right. "Cesar, you're scaring me."

My mind starts flipping back at the things Ky has done so far. Sneaking in my room. The fair. The notes. The flower he kept. He thought I left him because I didn't care. His crazy outburst and the shit he said. Patrick's busted face.

"I don't mean to scare you, but I'm not going to lie and tell you not to worry. Don't. Provoke. Ky."

I get out of the car and notice the guys smoking out front, nodding their heads to Cesar. They all stare at me with curiosity when I walk inside. I'm wearing a hoodie Ky bought me and left in my closet. It says Palm Angels in big white letters across the front with the matching sweatpants. It's comfortable, but I wonder why they keep looking at me, blowing clouds of smoke in the air every time the guys take a drag.

"Why are they looking at me?" I ask Cesar once we are inside the tattoo shop. It smells like antiseptic with the calming sound of the tattoo guns. There are three people seated on leather chaises getting inked, with only two chairs left unoccupied.

"Maybe it's because you're wearing a twelve-hundred-dollar Palm Angels outfit, Hermosa. And, of course, because you are walking in here with me, and I'm good-looking."

I laugh, trying to hide the shock. Twelve hundred bucks? Is Ky insane? I know Ky comes from money. I've been in his house and seen his car, but really? There are about twenty inside my closet with different names that I can't pronounce. I thought this was some off-brand you find at Walmart or Target, and he was being nice.

"At least I won't go home naked when they try to rip it off my body," I deadpan.

His eyes go dark. "They touch you and they're dead."

A guy with tattoos all over his skin and the side of his face walks up. "Cesar." He smiles. "What brings you by?"

Cesar grins and gives him a fist bump. "I brought a friend. She needs a cover-up." Cesar looks at me. "Show him."

I push up my sleeve and show him the two letters I need to be covered up with my fingers. The tattoo artist's eyes go wide and looks up at me. "Are you sure about that? The flowers are good work, and I could shade a dark one in with no problem, but"––he takes a deep breath––"I don't want any problems." He looks over at Cesar. I'm confused. What's the big deal?

"It's her body, Vincent. Her choice."

"Yeah, man, but..."

Cesar gives him a hard look, and Vincent raises his hand. "Fine. Fill this out, and it's two hundred."

Cesar hands me the paper and pen. He takes out two hundred dollars and gives them to the guy behind the desk.

"I'll pay you back," I whisper.

"I didn't ask," he replies, knowing there is no arguing with him.

I follow Vincent to his station. He preps the chair so I can take a seat. "Take the hoodie off and I'll get started."

I do as he asks, and I try not to think about the scars on my back, visible from the upper part of my black tank top. I push my hair over my back, hoping no one notices the raised red scars.

When Vincent returns with the stencil of a small dark daisy and sits down, he freezes. He looks behind me, and the air shifts. All the hairs on my arms rise. I turn my head, and my heart drops like I'm on one of the fair rides.

"What are you doing, princess?"

It's Ky.

He looks over after he removes his t-shirt. His ripped muscles move with the effort. Tattoos inked all over his body in different places. The one I can see clearly from where I'm sitting is the band-aid over his left pec. I lean back, and my gaze lands on Cesar standing behind me with a worried expression.

My eyes dart to his name on my forearm, being prepped with a tattoo stencil. Ky peers close. "That is not fair, is it?"

"How did you know I was here?" But I know the answer. Cesar.

"I know things. Like the fact you don't really want to do what you are about to."

"It's my choice, Ky."

"You chose to get it."

"That was before."

He nods, reaching over and grabbing a laminated sheet with different lettering styles, handing it to me. "Pick a style." I look at the different types, trying to understand why he wants me to pick one. Don't provoke him, Rubi.

I point at an Italian script in huge letters. "This one."

He hands the sheet to Vincent. "The one she picked. Right here." He taps right above the band-aid tattoo over his chest.

"What do you want?" Vincent asks, looking between me and Ky.

"Her name in big letters. RUBIANA."

What the fuck? Vincent looks at me and smiles nervously. "Alright." He slides the chair he's sitting on. "Let me--"

"No," he growls, causing Vincent to drop his hands. "She can get something else if she wants, but my name stays on her skin." Ky's gaze lands on mine. "I'm making it fair. You got mine. It is only fair I get yours." His eyes go soft when they land on my scars. He takes a seat in the chair opposite mine.

Vincent moves like his ass is on fire, preparing the area to get inked. "You don't have to," I say, but it all falls on deaf ears. No one pays attention to what I said.

Ky wants, and Ky gets. No questions asked.

"You should add to the list. There are plenty of names you can add there, you know."

Ky raises a brow. "Names?"

"Yep." I hop off the chair. "Jen, Nicole, the whole cheer squad. I'm sure you can think of a lot more."

Cesar steps forward, giving me the 'what the hell are you doing?' look, but I don't care. Ky wants to act like it's no big deal, and he could tattoo my name like it means something. He wasn't thinking of it when he called me names or burned down our tree house. The piece on my arm reminded me of the only thing I had good in my life. It was pure.

"I thought we were friends, Rubi?"

"We are, but not that kind."

He nods to Vincent to continue. "I think we were this afternoon when I spoon-fed you. On Tuesday night when--"

"Stop it," I warn.

He doesn't flinch when Vincent begins working on the tattoo. Not once. "Sit." He smiles from the corner of his mouth. "Pick something else if you want but you're not removing my name or the memory of me off your skin."

"What is he talking about, Rubi?" Cesar asks.

My eyes widen, pleading with Ky, but he isn't having it. "He doesn't know, does he, Rubi."

"Know what?" Cesar presses, looking between me and Ky.

"Me and Rubi go way back. Before--when we were kids."

Cesar looks at me with a confused expression on his handsome face. "You know him? How?"

"They took her from me, but she's here now."

"Stop talking crazy, Ky."

"I'm not crazy. Well... sometimes." He points to Cesar. "You should ask Cesar. He's lucky."

It feels like silence blankets the tattoo shop. The only sound came from the gun in Vincent's hand, tracing the outline of my name on Ky's skin.

"Why is he lucky?" I ask.

"Because he didn't know, Rubi. He didn't know about us. That is the only reason he's still breathing."

The entrance of the tattoo shop opens, and three guys walk in with tattoos all over their necks and arms. They look like gangbangers. Short haircuts, white tank tops, jeans, and gold chains. They all have the same look. Dangerous.

Ky nods at Cesar. Cesar moves to my side so Ky has a clear view from where he is sitting.

One of them gives me a once-over, making me want to shudder. I remember being around guys like this in foster care. Always looking at girls like they were a piece of meat. Openly gawking and licking their lips suggestively. You could almost see what was crossing their mind when they were doing it. Which was why they thought they could fuck you with or without your permission because no one would care.

Ky taps Vincent to stop and slides a gun from the back of his jeans, placing it on his lap. Holy shit. Ky has a gun. He gives the guy staring at me a murderous glare. "Look at her one more time, and I'll blow your fucking head off," he warns. "I suggest you get the fuck out of here if you want to keep breathing."

The guy and his two friends raise their hands. "I don't want any problems. I-I know who you are. I didn't mean any disrespect," he says nervously, walking backward out the way they came.

Cesar walks forward with a gun aimed at their foreheads.

"Good. I'm glad we understand each other," Ky says, relaxed. Like it is normal for him to scare away gangsters threatening them with their lives.

Vincent begins again on the tattoo. "She your girl?" Vincent asks.

"No," I quip.

Ky smiles. "Yeah, she's always been my girl."

"Stop, Ky."

But I know he won't. It's true what Cesar said in the car. In Ky's mind, I belong to him in some weird way. He is obsessed with me. Everyone's warning repeated inside my head.

"I'm going home."

"That's not a good idea right now, Rubi."

I pinch my brows together. "Why not?" I ask looking at Cesar when he walks back inside.

"Your half-brother fucked up." He chuckles. "It isn't safe for you to go to the house and stay there alone."

"I have to go back."

"You will, but not tonight."

"Why?"

He scrapes his teeth on his bottom lip. "Because I don't trust them... with you."

"Let me guess, I'm safe with you."

"You will always be safe with me. Even when we were ten years old, you were safe with me. You just didn't know it."

I glance at Cesar and watch as realization crosses his features. The boy I told him about. The one everyone thought I had made up. The boy who was my best friend and the daisies I loved so much––the reason I have them tattooed all over my right arm.

When Vincent finishes Ky's tattoo, I get a small one. The stem of a daisy with a single petal, like the one I left him all those years ago, on the top of my hand by my thumb.

———

After Vincent is done, I wince when he places the clear plastic over it. I feel warm fingers softly slide my hair behind my ear. "It will only sting a little on the hand like a small burn," Ky says softly. "It's a sensitive spot." I nod and look at the small tattoo, wondering why it stung so much for being so small, but I like it.

"Thank you, Vincent."

"Anytime, Rubi."

Ky fishes out the money Cesar paid Vincent and hands it to Cesar, but he shakes his head. "It's all good, man. I'm good."

"Take it," Ky says in a hard tone.

Cesar nods, knowing there is no arguing. It feels weird being alone with both of them, but Cesar is my friend. He will always be my friend, and I won't let Ky hurt him.

"I need to talk to you," I tell Ky, walking outside, noticing his black BMW parked next to Cesar's car.

He leans on his car, placing his shirt over his head. Thank God. His hard muscles were distracting.

"What is it?"

I look over at Cesar, watching him inside his car and then back at him. "You have to promise me that you won't hurt Cesar." I can see his lips twitch in amusement. "This isn't funny, Ky. I need you to promise me."

He angles his head. "You want me to promise not to hurt the guy that works for me and so happens to be the guy that got to fuck you."

I shake my head. "Is that a problem?"

"Fuck, Rubi. You fucked him."

"And not you, right?" I scoff. "That's what this is about."

He rolls his eyes, and before I take it back, I blurt, "Fine." His eyes narrow. "If that is the big issue, then fine. I'll sleep with you."

His nostrils flare. "Don't play games with me. I've been patient with you."

"Who said it was a game? But you have to promise me you will protect him. He is on his own, and you know it. I know he chose this life, but I can't let him die from it."

He snorts. "How noble of you."

"Why are you such an ass?"

He pushes off his car and steps closer. "You're pushing me, Rubi. I'll make him watch while you're on top riding me."

My pussy throbs, but I call his bluff. "You wouldn't."

He smiles. "You're right. You're beautiful, and I couldn't stomach another man watching you while you take my cock. "

"I'm not beautiful."

"To me, there is nothing more beautiful than you, Rubi. Not even the scars on your back, because those are mine. Your scars mean more than anything in my life. More than life itself."

I look up so the tears cresting on my lashes don't spill. "They're ugly. You don't have to lie."

"Let me show you."

"Show me what?" I counter. "What a freak I am, so you could make fun of me with Jen or Nicole when you compare me to them."

"There was this girl," he says, opening the passenger door. "I met her when I was ten years old." He pauses. Then, continues, "When she left, I forgot to tell her how I felt about her. The secret I kept from her when we would play our game. But she kept a big secret from me...the one that showed me how much she loved being with me before I could tell her I loved her."

My heart is in my throat because I felt the same way. I would do anything to be with him, but there is so much hate between us-- so much confusion about who we are to each other.

"But you hated me more for so long. That is why I asked Cesar to bring me here, to erase what I thought was love. The same way you destroyed everything you hated, including me. You erased the place where we shared those special moments."

I slide inside the car, and he shuts the door. "Take me to your house," I tell him when he fires up the car.

He looks over and gestures for Cesar to put his window down. "I'll catch up with you later. Thanks for looking out."

He means thanks for telling me she contacted you.

"Always," he responds. Then he leans forward and glances at me through the window. "I'll see you later. You can call me. You know that, right?"

"I know." He begins to pull out of the parking space. "Be careful," I rush out before he pulls away.

"I'll make sure nothing happens to him," Ky says quietly on the way to his house.

"Don't lie to me, Ky. I saw the look in your eyes when you entered the tattoo shop."

"That I want to fuck him up for touching you, yeah. But I can't because that would hurt you, Rubi, and I'm tired of people hurting you-- including me."

I look down at the tattoo on my hand, hoping he means it. "Thank you."

CHAPTER TEN
Ky

IF THERE WAS anything I could do to make her happy, I would. It breaks me to see that she doesn't trust me. I see the worried look in her eye when I walk into the same room. It pains me to see it, but there is nothing I can do to change who I am or what I will become.

As I got older, I began to understand the reason for my existence. The reason my mother left me and my father. It was because my grandfather was the head of the Italian mafia. My father married my mother against his family's wishes. They didn't approve of my mother because she didn't approve of my father's way of life. But he loved her and moved here to start a life.

He started a dynasty with Chris and Tyler's fathers in the U.S. When I came along, it changed everything. I was part of something bigger but kept hidden away from my father's family.

When my grandfather learned I was born, my mother left my father. She didn't look back when I watched her go. In her eyes, I was already one of them. She was right, but loyalty is everything in the mafia. My mother betrayed my father in more ways than one. After that, my father warned me to never let a woman mess with my head. The problem was I was already fucked up.

I trap my bottom lip with my teeth when I park my car in front of my house. Another thing I was given from my father's side of the family. My father waited until I turned eighteen to leave me on my own. He stops by to check up on me periodically to make sure things are running smoothly.

Rubi exits the car and hurriedly walks up to the front door.

Her gorgeous strawberry-blonde hair fell around her shoulders. The designer joggers, not hiding the amazing curve of her ass.

I raise my brow, pressing the code on the front door. "You need to pee?"

She steps inside. "No."

"Then why..."

She pushes me against the wall, slamming the front door. Her body melted against mine. Fuck. Her fingers tug on my hair. Her hungry mouth was on my neck. I grip her face in both my hands and crash my mouth against hers. She smells of lavender and vanilla.

I pick her up by her thighs, her legs wrapping around my waist, and turn, pushing her against the wall. I kiss her hard. Our tongues dance, my hard dick pushing up against the crotch of her joggers.

"Fuck me, Ky."

"Is that what you want, Rubi? For me to fuck your tight cunt."

"Yes," she hisses, grinding her hot pussy on my cock.

I've held myself back from taking more. If I fuck her, there's no turning back. She will belong to me, and God help whoever gets in my way.

"There is no turning back, Rubi. Not for me."

Her eyes are full of want. Floating on the need for release. But I need to be sure. She needs to be sure.

Her pussy grinds on my cock in response, and I swear I almost come on the spot. I pin on her the wall and slide my hand in her panties, feeling her wet clit. Fuck, she's wet.

"Ky, please," she cries softly.

I kiss the spot under her ear and slide a finger into her hot cunt. "Tell me you want my cock, Rubi."

"I want your cock, Ky. I want it deep inside me."

I close my eyes, imagining her tight pussy milking me while I fuck her. I swirl my finger over her clit and add a second finger. She's tight. Ripe and wet. I slide my fingers out and grip her thighs, ascending the stairs toward my room.

I lay her on my bed. "If you want me to stop, this is the time to tell me, Rubi."

She removes the sweater along with her top. Her pretty breasts sit high. Her pink nipples begging for my tongue. Gorgeous. She's perfect. But there is only one way she would believe me if I told her.

She gasps when I flip her around, pulling her pants and panties off in one go. She's on all fours on the mattress. Her round ass and wet pussy ready for me. I take off my shirt and kick my jeans and boxers off. The only thing left is the plastic wrap on my fresh tattoo with her name inked across my chest.

"Ky?"

She's worried about her scars. I can hear it in the tone of her voice. I slide her hair to the side and trace her raised red scars with the tip of my finger, memorizing them and imagining the pain she endured.

Our pain.

She turns her head over her shoulder, and our eyes meet for a second before my lips touch her raised skin in a soft kiss. "There is no part of you I don't find beautiful, Rubi. Your scars are mine." The head of my cock brushes over her wet aching slit. "This pussy is mine." My cock crowns her entrance.

She thinks our love when we were kids ended. She doesn't know it turned into something fierce, like a burning twin flame. Once ignited again, there is no extinguishing it. Nothing could stop it from consuming us both. "I love you, Rubiana. I'll always love you," I whisper before shoving my cock inside her deep like she wanted.

Her back arches against my chest. I wrap my hand around her throat, shunting my hips.

"Ky," she breathes. "You're so big." I close my eyes because she is so tight. I'm afraid to move. I'm afraid to hurt her.

When I feel her body relax, I begin to fuck her. Slow at first. Then hard.

I fuck her hard and deep. Her sweat moans are beautiful like I imagined them in my dreams. The way I imagined them when she thought I hated her.

It's easy to say you hate someone you love because you don't want to let them go. I could never let her go. There is no me without her. Like there is a flower without water or the sun. The sun is where we grow, where we both burn for each other. The sun will set and rise every day because without it--without her, I don't exist.

My tongue trails her scars, licking her wounds while grinding my cock deep inside her. Owning her.

I pull out of her pussy. I flip her over, her legs spread wide, her pink pussy swollen, begging to be sucked. Later.

I place her hands on her wrists above her head, careful I don't touch the tattoo on her hand.

She's quiet. Like she's taking it all in. As I am. The crossroads of where we met, how we thought we ended, only to find each other and start over.

"We didn't use a condom," she says, but I never planned to. Not with her. Not ever.

"I know." I push inside her, and we both groan. She feels too perfect. Too good, but I always knew she would.

Her hands slide down the dips of my abs and back up to my neck. I place my elbows on the bed, cradling her face. "I want you to look at me when I'm inside you."

I grind harder and faster. I dip my head and lick her nipple and then the other snaking my tongue up her neck until I take her mouth. The palms of her hands slide down my back, gripping my ass, pushing me deeper, and I smile against her lips.

"More," she begs.

"You want more, baby?"

She nods.

I raise her knees to her chest, and I take her hard. Fucking her. Pounding her.

"Yes...fuck...yes."

Her pussy is wet. The wet sounds her pussy makes bringing me to the edge. The feel of her tight pussy gripping my cock. Her neck arches and I know she's close. Our bodies are slick with sweat, my balls slapping against her ass.

"I'm going to come, Ky," she says between our mingled breaths.

I bite my lip, trying to hold on. "Me too."

"Please, don't stop."

"Never."

She lets out a loud moan. "Mm....yes." Her pussy squeezes my cock, her blunt nails dig into my skin, and she falls apart, her orgasm slamming into her.

Her face is gorgeous when she comes for me. I'm fascinated by her. All of her. Her eyes are glazed. Her lips parted, but I didn't stop. I cup her face with my hands, my thumb caressing her bottom lip.

"I'm going to come inside you," I say softly.

Her eyes go wide, and I come hard, seeing stars behind my eyes when I spill inside her with a groan. Sweat drips down my abs to the part where we were joined. I open my eyes, find hers, and whisper, "You're mine."

Chapter Eleven
Rubi

HE WHISPERED HE LOVED ME, and my heart melted. I thought he meant it in the past-tense when he said the words outside the tattoo shop.

He said I was beautiful, and the way he kissed my scars, I knew he meant it when I heard him say it again. Every word. I couldn't tell him I loved him because I wasn't sure if I trusted him. I was scared. What's love without trust? A dead-end street with a promise of heartbreak. I never thought having sex with Ky would be like this. There wasn't much I could compare him to, but this was different. The way he touched me. The way he made me feel beautiful. I know me sleeping with Ky changes everything. I just hope I can survive the fall.

The sun rises on the horizon, lighting up the room. I reach out next to me, and the bed is empty. When I sit up, I hear the shower running, and I smile.

I pad my way to his ensuite, the glass shower fogged up and open the shower door. Finding Ky's hard body dripping wet with his cock in his hand.

He's hard, eyes hooded, shamelessly stroking his cock.

"Is that for me?" I ask.

His tongue peaks out, water dripping down his chin. His eyes trailing up my body. "It's always been you, Rubi." I watch his hand stroke his cock. "You were sleeping so peacefully. I didn't want to wake you."

I enter the marble shower and shut the door behind me with a thud.

Ky's arm muscles ripple with every stroke of his hand over his dick. I kneel in front of him. My eyes look up. I've never taken a man's cock inside my mouth.

I swallow hard. The mist of the water spraying over my naked body. His eyes lower. "You've never done this, have you?"

I shake my head. My stomach flutters when he smiles. "Good. I want nothing more than to be the only cock that has fucked your mouth. The only one that has cum inside your body. But..."

"Is..." I lick my lips, struggling with my words. "Did you mean what you said last night?"

He lifts my chin with his finger. His eyes were hungry but guarded. "Every word. But I need you to trust me, Rubi." He lifts me so I'm standing facing his chest. "I know you don't trust me, and I'm not going to mess this up. It's not about sex or childhood revenge." He swallows. "Not anymore. This is something bigger."

My eyes trail the letters on his chest spelling my name. "I don't understand."

"You will... in time."

Ky drove me to school after our shower. I wish I could say that I see the sun brighter and hear the birds chirping after the night we had. The words spoken that I didn't have in me to return, but he was right. I didn't trust him.

Loyalty is, as far as I can see.

I ignore the stares and the whispers when I walk the halls. Even Jen, Nicole, and her crew. I ignore it all, thinking about what Ky said. That this is something bigger. I don't know what he was talking about, but he knows something I don't. Something I can't see.

"Where were you last night?" I look up from the bleachers and see Tyler's angry expression.

"Out," I chirp.

"With Ky?"

I nod. "Yeah, with Ky, but you already knew that so why are you asking me questions you know the answers to?"

"Because I don't get you. I have repeatedly told you to stay away, and the first thing you do is stay with him." His eyes narrow to slits. "You fucked him, didn't you?"

I drop the sandwich on my plate. "What, you're the pussy police now?"

He snorts, looking up and shaking his head. "You fell for his shit. I can't believe it."

"Fell for what?" I sneer.

What is his problem?

"His games. You think you're the first he's messed with. The first one he manipulates with his lies. The first one he takes is his fancy car. The first one he takes to his house to fuck."

"I think you need to watch your mouth, brother." My head turns, watching Ky stop in front of Tyler.

Tyler straightens. His fists clenched at his side. "Or what?"

Ky gives him a rubbery grin that disappears, making all the tiny hairs on my arms stand despite the sun sitting high in the blue sky.

"None of this will end well, Tyler. I fuck you up, nothing happens. You try to touch me, and everything will, and I can guarantee it won't end in your favor. You, warning me off, Rubi, is like spitting in my food," he says with a dangerous edge to his tone. He leans close. "You can tell your daddy I said that."

Tyler's nose flairs like a bull, but something holds him back. Something Ky knows that I don't, but Tyler does. The problem is I need to figure out who to trust.

"Why do you have a problem with me being with Ky?"

He shakes his head, but his eyes are blank. "I don't want you to get hurt."

Ky chuckles. "Yeah, keep telling yourself that." And turns around, walking away.

I get up. "Ky?"

He holds his hand up but doesn't stop. "I'll take you home after school, principessa."

"He's going to hurt you, Rubi," Tyler says, taking a seat next to me. "That's what he does. He destroys."

"I've been taking care of myself for a long time, Tyler. I don't need a guardian angel. I don't need a savior."

"Someone needs to be," he mutters.

"What was that?"

"I said someone needs to be!" He repeats, raising his voice.

I let out a sarcastic laugh. "You know, when I met you. You couldn't stand the sight of me..."

"I know, but things change."

"Nothing has changed. I'm still Rubi. The bastard child that disrupts your little perfect life in suburbia."

"He didn't know..."

I sit up. Anger running through my veins at how stupid he sounds. "Of course, he knew, Tyler. If you expect me to believe he didn't know. If they contacted him because I was going to jail, then you really are stupid. It wasn't the first time I was caught. He knew where I was." His eyes widen. "I'm not stupid, Tyler. I was on the other side of town the whole time..."

"And Ky? You expect me to believe there isn't something more you aren't telling me about you two?"

I blink back tears, pulling my arm out of my school jacket and showing him my forearm. His eyes find mine. Putting the pieces together. "Ky is the boy, Tyler. The one they thought didn't exist." I let the tears fall.

He closes his eyes. "Fuck."

I slide my arm back in and fix my jacket, not regretting that I told him. It would be better if it came from me. He should know so he understands. For me. For Ky. And for him.

"I'm sorry I didn't tell you sooner."

He hangs his head. "It makes sense. The way he acted when he saw you. What he just said." He slides his hand over his face.

"What do you mean?"

He turns to look at me, but the look in his eyes frightens me. "There is no way he will let you go, Rubi."

I scoff. "So, I've heard."

He turns to face me, holding my arms. "Rubi, obsession it-- it's like a drug. You can't help it. It's all you think about. You keep

100

coming back. Again and again. You don't stop. You can't–– he can't. And he won't. You, of all people, know what a drug is like. What it does. How it consumes. What Ky has for you, Rubi. It's stronger than obsession and love combined. It's something else." He gets up.

I shield my eyes from the sun's glare and ask, "Like?"

"Madness. What he feels for you is madness."

"How do you know that?"

But I knew he was telling the truth. I wanted to see if he could make sense of it.

"Because I've known him a long time, and he has never looked at a girl the way he looks at you. Like you're everything that he sees, and nothing or no one matters. "

CHAPTER TWELVE
Rubi

FOR THE PAST TWO WEEKS, Ky has dropped me off at home every day after school. Since my father and Tyler's mother come home from work late, they don't see the black BMW dropping me off in the driveway. But when you get away with doing something for so long, you start to test the limit. You stop caring what anyone thinks.

It's one week until Halloween. Decorations are all over the school and on people's front lawns. The air smells like fall. Different than what I'm used to. Where I come from, decorations placed outside were stolen within a day. It wasn't the kind you bought but the kind you made. You would be surprised what you could make with free school supplies given to you by donors, but when you put all the time into making something, you can pass the time, and it gets stolen. You stopped making them, and holidays like Halloween were just another day. The only thing I looked forward to was the free candy.

"What are you thinking about?"

I watch the houses with fancy decorations and inflatables for fall or Halloween through the window. Some homes are decorated with both like they couldn't decide between a fake graveyard or pumpkins with hay. Or the inflatable skeleton or the pumpkin with a turkey behind it. Some people find it stupid. Hell, some kids think it's dumb. But when you come from nothing––had nothing, you learn to appreciate it.

"Nothing. I'm admiring all the Halloween and fall decorations people have put out. "

"Do you like Halloween?"

I shrug and smile, admiring how Ky's hand grips the steering wheel. "I like the free candy."

He arches a brow. "Free candy?"

I lay my head on the headrest. "When you're hungry all the time. You begin to love certain words."

"Like?"

I laugh. "Words like free candy. Free food. Complimentary. All you can eat."

"Did you ever dress up?"

"I tried a bed sheet once when I was eight," I reply like I crushed a snail with my shoe.

"A sheet? What kind of sheet?"

"An old bedsheet that had ugly patterns on it. It wasn't white, but I wanted to get free candy on Halloween, and I couldn't exactly show up at someone's house with a grocery bag I found on the street without a costume, shouting trick or treat. So, I grabbed the sheet off my bed. It was dirty with ugly green and teal stripes on it. My mother found it on the curb when someone was evicted. Anyway, I cut two holes to see through it and put it over my head. I went door to door, holding a used grocery bag. There were no decorations where we lived with my mother, but I didn't care." I half shrugged. "It never hurt to try. Anyway, I was made fun of and had a couple of doors slam in my face, but I got some. I walked so much and knocked on so many doors I had the entire grocery backfilled with candy. I was so happy. I couldn't stop eating it all on my way home."

"Your favorite is chocolate."

I smile. "Yeah, that was how I knew what different candies tasted like. At least the chocolate ones it was the only kind I could try. When I made it home, my stepfather took it from me and shared it with all the people in the house and didn't give it back. He said my teeth would rot." I sigh. "I told him I didn't eat dinner because my mother was high and passed out on the couch, so how was that possible. He hit me across the face and dragged me by the hair, shoving me inside my room."

"I'm sorry."

I shake my head because it wasn't his fault. There is nothing for him to be sorry about.

"It's not your fault, Ky. You know, every day I'm here. I compare. I compare my life then to what it is now. The school, where I sleep, and where I eat."

He stops at a red light. "And?"

"And none of it feels like home."

"Because it's not." He shakes his head, waving his hand at the neighborhood before us. "None of this is home if the people with you don't love you. If they don't care about you."

He's right. Mansion. Crack house. Group home. It's not a home if the people living with you don't care or love you.

"You're right."

"But I love you, Rubi." My heart squeezes, and my stomach flips like it did when we were kids. Like it did, when he was inside me and he said it.

The light turns green, and he drives onto his street. "I know you don't believe me, but I do." He stops in front of the three-car garage.

"Do you think mom and dad's—— when they kiss is gross?" I ask.

His dark eyes watch me picking out the daisies like he knows all the answers to my questions before I ask.

"When I grow up, I want to be with a girl, and I want to be a daddy. I want her to be a mom. I would kiss her because I like her and she likes me. So, no, it's not. It's normal. I smile because I want to be that girl and live in a house like this one. "It's my turn."

He grabbed the five daisies from my hands so we could begin. I want to tell him that it's not fair, but I know it is. I asked a question before our game started, so it was his turn. After the last petal, I smile because I won anyway, and it's my turn to ask.

"Don't lie." He leans back on his hands, his dark hair over his brow. His thick lashes frame dark eyes like the darkness of my closet. My safe place.

"I can't tell the truth if you don't ask the question."

I twirl my fingers in my lap, sitting cross-legged on the wood slats under our tree. "Alright, you want kids when you grow up?" He nods. "So, you sayin the girl would be the same one that gets to ride around with you in your dream car. The one you want. Like Batman." He nods again, and I lick my lips. "Who is she? The girl that you want to be with? The one that gets to be the mommy."

I look at my dirty fingernails, wishing mine were clean like his. I wish I smelled good enough so I could be that girl, hoping it's me he thinks about in that way.

Butterflies swarm in my stomach, waiting for him to answer. The little flutters I always get when I'm near him. His fingers move the stems of the other four daisies between his fingers. I blink once, twice, and when I think my little heart will stop beating, he says, "You. It will always be you, Rubi. No matter what. You're my best friend. You're my girl."

I watch him press the button. The first door goes up, and I blink several times, recognizing the taillights on the shiny black car like the picture in his bedroom. His dream car.

He turns his head. "I kept my promise, Rubi. I've never taken another girl in my dream car."

"Like Batman," I whisper.

The car roars to life. I grin when he makes sure I'm buckled in in the sleek black Lamborghini. He places the car in gear. "Ready?" I nod.

He takes me to dinner at a small Italian restaurant and lets me order whatever I want. Before my father and Caroline make it home, he stops at a grocery store.

"What are we doing here?" I ask.

"You'll see," he says, opening my door.

I follow him inside. The smell of fruits and fresh bread permeates the air, reminding me of when I was a kid; I would take a piece of fruit and eat it before walking out without paying for it. I hoped that one day, I could fill a grocery cart full of groceries and have the money to pay for it. It was the first time I took food without paying for it. It became a norm at the group home, risking myself so the younger kids could eat. It must feel good when you have money to pay for simple things like food and clothes because taking without paying for it felt horrible.

Ky turns right, stopping at the candy aisle. "Okay," he says, picking up a few bars of chocolate. He finds a shopping basket in the corner and picks it up, dropping them all inside. "Pick whatever you want, Rubi."

Tears prick my eyes. "I-I don't have that much money on me."

"I didn't ask that. I've told you not to worry about money. Not with me. Not ever."

There are so many rows and a selection of different kinds. Gum, chocolates, sour candy, sweet candy. There is so much to choose and some I've never heard of before.

I take one, thinking to myself to keep the limit at five. Ky walks away and returns with another shopping basket with the same black handles and begins picking one of each.

"What are you doing?"

He grabs one from each row. One after another, filling the basket. "What does it look like? I'm buying my girl candy. All the candy."

"You can't."

"I can and I will. Keep telling me the stories, Rubi. I'll keep filling in the blanks."

On our way back, with the huge bag of candy sitting between my feet, I open one and pop it in my mouth, letting the sour goodness explode on my tongue. "These are good," I say with a smile. I swallow, holding up the package, and read, "Sour patch."

"I'm glad you like them."

"Thank you," I say quietly. "For dinner and the candy." And I meant it.

This is the side of Ky I fell for. The side of him I remember when we were kids. It is the side that few people get to see, and it is the only side I want to see. The side that tells me, he's mine.

He pulls up to my father's house, and the front door opens. My father steps out, looks at the car, and watches Ky walk around and open my door. When I step out, Ky follows behind me. My father's eyes narrow on the bags.

"I told you that if you didn't follow my rules, what would happen."

"I do follow the rules. I don't go out with guys you think I'm not good enough for. I make it home before curfew. I go to school and come back. What's the problem?"

He points at Ky. "He is the problem. Him with you."

"Oh, I'm not good enough for Ky either," I grit. "So, who am I good for?"

"Get inside, Rubiana."

"No."

"Get inside!"

"Talk to her like that one more time..."

"Or what, Ky. Huh? Or what?"

Ky steps up to my father, making him step back. Ky has about two inches on him.

A hand pulls the door open wider, and Tyler appears in the doorway, looking between me and Ky. Then, at my dad. "Dad, what is going on..."

"Tell him, Dad," Ky mocks with a menacing smile. "What is going on?"

My father grunts, staring down at Ky. You can feel the tension in the air like a dark cloud moving in. "I don't want you around my daughter."

"Why?" I ask. "Why not?"

"Because I said so. I'm the parent."

I laugh sarcastically. "Great timing, Stephen. Where were you for the last seventeen years and a half, huh? Where were you when I was hungry?" My father flinches like I struck him. "What's wrong?" I taunt.

"Out! I want you out. You're going back."

"Dad," Tyler calls out, but he isn't listening. His brown eyes are filled with regret. He regrets me.

I nod, but I'm dying inside. Rejection is a shitty pill to swallow. It's like kicking a helpless dog, then throwing them out after you hurt them and have nowhere to go.

Ky gets closer, looking down at my father with murder in his eyes. "Take it back." He jabs his finger at Stephen's chest. "Take it back now!" He roars.

"No. I'm calling them tomorrow. She's going back."

"Dad, don't do this." Tyler pleads.

"Man, fuck you!" Ky roars and grabs my hand. "Rubi, get Hope and your stuff."

"She can't leave with you," my father warns.

Ky gives him a vicious smile. "Call them, and I will end you. She is going to be staying with me."

"That's not gonna happen, Ky. You're not above the law, and she is my responsibility until she finishes high school." Stephen looks at me. "Then, you are on your own. If you want to do whatever you want, then fine. Like you said, once you graduate, you're gone."

My heart is in my throat. Fuck him. I knew his claws would come out sooner or later.

"Don't bother. I'm leaving now. Call whoever the fuck you want to call."

I push past Stephen and Tyler and walk into the house. Caroline is sitting at the dining table with tears in her eyes. She looks up. "I'm so sorry, Rubi. If it were up..."

"Save it. I don't need your pity. I never wanted it. You can live in your house full of lies. You better hope it doesn't bury your husband."

I'm feeling like shit. I want to scream and hurt someone, and I know she doesn't deserve it, but I can't help myself. I get why Stephen married her. He preys on the weak, which is what she is: weak. Fragile. And he's a monster hiding in the closet.

CHAPTER THIRTEEN
Ky

I WALK INSIDE MY HOUSE, slamming the front door, trying to keep myself from going back and stabbing her father between the eyes, knowing I couldn't do it because that would make me a natural-born killer.

I slam the refrigerator door closed after grabbing a beer, trying to formulate a plan. I couldn't bring her here with no room inside the Lamborghini. Where would I put the cat and all her stuff? I didn't want to leave her there, but I had no choice. And the way I'm feeling, I wanted to strangle Stephen for what he said to her. Words Rubi doesn't deserve. Words a girl like her doesn't need to hear.

I lean on the stainless-steel door, trying to wrap my head around his sudden change of heart. Stephen doesn't want me around Rubi. That much is obvious. He wants her gone, but why?

"I've been expecting you."

I turn around. My father is sitting in the dark living room on the single armchair.

As if my night couldn't get any worse.

"Did Stephen call to tattle tale?"

"He did." He crosses his leg over the other at the ankles. "He wants you to stay away from Rubi, but we already discussed this."

"He wants to talk to the judge so that Rubi could serve the remainder of her sentence. He wants her gone."

"He wants Tyler to take over. If she's in jail and tried as an adult, he wouldn't need her to sign anything. Not that she was going to, given her background. A billion-dollar stake in a conglomerate is hard to pass up. He went to the lawyers. They said one of the stipulations with the board would not allow anyone to have a stake in the company if they didn't have moral character. A junkie for a mother and a record for stealing is not in her favor. They could overlook the mother being a meth addict but not the jail time for stealing."

Motherfucker.

"So, you're telling me that he prefers to ruin his daughter's life so that he could ensure his son's future is protected. Why?"

"Because she was a mistake, Ky. Her mother trapped him by getting pregnant. He doesn't want her to inherit what he's helped build. He wants to leave it all to his son. His legacy through him."

I snort. "You mean what you allowed him to build. Like you said, my history. Your family. What if I want her to be part of it?"

"It's not that simple, Ky. Women in our world are only major players if born into it. Rubi is illegitimate and is just a partner in a company I built. He's not in the mafia but has connections. If he wants her to disappear, Ky, he will make that happen, and there is no leverage for you to stop it. There is no reason for anyone to get involved. She's no one."

"To me, she is!"

I hate raising my voice to my father. Since my mother left, he's shown me what I'm a part of. What Chris and Tyler can imagine but don't know about or who my grandfather is in the Italian mafia. I'm the hidden prince of the mafia world. My father was a mafia king hiding me from the lions and raising me with wolves.

"I know, son. It is why I haven't gotten involved. Until now. I can't let this get in the way of business." He sits up in the chair. "She will be in danger, and you will start a war. Stephen doesn't know everything, and when he does, he will think he has more leverage. He will use her against you. Then, people will die. Because you are who you are."

He's right. Stephen has me by the balls, But I made her a

promise. I'm the only one she could trust. When I told her I loved her, I meant it.

"I'm not going to give her up. Don't ask me to do that because you know I won't."

"I know, and that is why I came." He pinches the bridge of his nose. "You need to listen to what I'm going to tell you very carefully." I take a pull from my beer and sit on the bar stool by the island, bracing myself for what he will say next because I know I am not going to like it.

"I can pay off the judge so that he can make the jail time go away, but..."

There is always a fucking but.

"But?"

"She needs to lay low. If Stephen thinks you are with her, he will make her disappear. She's a risk. Like I said, if we go the other route, people will die, and most likely, they will get rid of her anyway, thinking she is just a loose end."

He's right. I don't like it. I want to scream. I want to break everything in this empty fucking house, but that will not save Rubi. It will not get what I want. Her.

"She doesn't have anyone––Where would she go? She is packing her things as we speak."

"I know you will not like what I say next, but I don't see any other way. She can stay with Caesar."

I feel like I've been kicked in the throat. Jealousy claws my insides turning them into shit.

"You're asking me to let the girl I love live with the man who slept with her first? A man who has looked me in the eye and told me he loves her. He's backed off because he thinks he isn't good enough because of the life he chose. You're asking me to take her to a house where there are drugs and people fucking in the next room on the side of town where she was raised by meth addicts."

"I know, son, but she can't stay here with you. And Stephen cannot find out you are with her. Let him give Tyler his control. Let the board vote him in."

"And then what?"

"Then, you both would have graduated and can take her wherever you wish. She will be free. But if you get involved now, you will put her in danger and draw attention to yourself."

Meaning my grandfather would want me to take my seat in his circle. As his grandson. A life that my mother wanted me to be free of. A life my father had to go back into. There are no daisies. There are no treehouses. All there is is drugs, power, control, and bloodshed. Making everyone in your life a target––Making Rubi a target.

"What about school?"

"Finish the year playing the role of Ky, the playboy." I shake my head. "I'm not going to hurt her. I won't make her think I chose another girl over her."

"I'm not saying to stick your cock in another girl, Ky. That is up to you. But if you love her, you have to play the role to save her from her family. I know she already bears the scars of her sacrifice for you, and I know what it means to have her live at that house, but it's your territory, Ky. You control all of it."

"What about her going to school here?"

My father shakes his head. Dread snakes up my spine.

"She needs to transfer to the West Park public high school."

"Fuck!" I throw the beer bottle across the room, hearing the glass shatter, mirroring exactly how I feel, pulling the strands of my hair.

"They will eat her up there. It's full of gangsters and drug dealers."

"The ones you control, Ky. No one will touch her. You know that, and so will everyone there. It's not forever."

"What if she says no? What if she leaves me again?"

"She won't."

I turn with tears in my eyes, hating myself for feeling power-less. "How do you know that?"

He gets up and puts his hands on my shoulders. "Because that young girl loves you. The scars on her back. The pain she took for you at such a young age just to see you. My son. That...is loyalty,

114

Ky. That is love. She is not your mother. She isn't going to leave you. I know that now."

I don't want her there. I don't want her in that house with things that remind her of her past.

"Let me talk to my grandfather. I'll leave with you right now."

But my father shakes his head, and I know what he will say. That I have to choose that life and it's not a guarantee. Money is what matters in this world.

"Money is everything in our world. You know that. There is money at stake. It is why Stephen wants her gone. He doesn't want the board to know of her existence. The paperwork had all his information when she was at her hearing, and he was afraid she would figure out who her father was and how much he was worth. Demand money or worse... That she was his daughter and firstborn. She would be entitled to his estate by law since he ruled out his wife. It's the same thing we discussed after the pool incident. Tyler is about to turn eighteen and graduate."

"Why, though? Why does he want her out now? "

"I don't know. He told me to warn you off because of the business and that he would call the social worker and the judge. I can work it out with the court."

"Who will be her guardian?"

"No one. She's eighteen. I just need to pay off the judge to make the probation sentence disappear. She won't get a diploma from West Lake Prep, but she will graduate. And... she has you."

One of his bodyguards walks inside the house wearing a black suit. He folds is hands, waiting for further instruction from my father, and I notice my family's mark tattooed on his neck. The one they give all trusted bodyguards, a little star that signifies their rank.

My father looks up and nods in his direction. He stands up. "Take her to Cesar's. There is a driver in a black Escalade outside to pick her up. I'll take care of the rest. Her enrollment and the other details we discussed."

He walks away, and I have never felt more helpless. More disgusted.

When his security detail walks outside, my father turns back around. He must see the anguish in my eyes. The look of defeat in my expression. "This is you loving her, Ky. You are fighting for her the way she fought to be with you. Look at the positive side of things. She is all yours, just on the other side of town."

Yeah, we're all her demons live. And I'm the one dropping her off.

CHAPTER FOURTEEN
Rubi

I HAVE MOVED to different places, and none felt permanent. None were safe. It was replacing one hell for another. Every place I went, no one wanted me. No one loved me enough. No one cared enough about me. Not my mother or my father.

Ky told me what my father planned and what his father suggested. How he was going to make sure my probation went away. A fresh start after I graduate.

However, I had to transfer schools to West Lake Public High School to finish the remainder of my senior year on Monday? It didn't matter what I thought or how I felt about it. It was my only option. Like everything, I had to accept every situation I've been given.

Knock. Knock.

"Rubi?"

"Come in."

The white door opens, and Hope runs under the twin bed that squeaks every time I move on it. I swear, whoever screws in this thing, it will sound like you are in a band.

"Are you okay? Do you need anything?"

"No, Cesar. I'm good."

I wince when the music starts again, drowning out the voices outside. Ky told me about the parties. The ones he warned me to stay out of. I'm grateful I have a roof over my head. I get to finish school, and there is no curfew. I'm free under the condition I have to graduate high school.

So, I have been holed up in the room for the past two days

since Ky dropped me off. I know what goes on in these places. Drugs. Sex and a mixture of both. This is the side Cesar warned me about. The side he didn't want me to be around, given my history of being raised by addicts.

"I can order you food? Whatever you want?" He pulls out his phone. The light from the screen illuminated his attractive face. "Ky gave me a list of all the things you like. Candy. The type of pizza. Chinese food."

My eyes sting. Ky's cold demeanor hurt. He dropped me off and left the instructions with Cesar. He didn't kiss me goodbye. The guys in Cesar's crew helped me with my stuff. He dropped me off like a dog you take to a shelter when the owner no longer wants it.

"I'm not hungry."

I lay on the bed with my knees to my chest.

"You need to eat, Rubi."

I snort. "I'm used to not eating, Cesar. It's really no big deal, but thanks anyway."

Someone buying me anything is the last thing I want. I want to get a job. I'm hoping Cesar will help me find one.

"Do you want to talk about it?"

I hear a giggle. I look up, and he's standing in the doorway with his white t-shirt and tattoos on every inch of his arms and neck. A girl in a short dress barely covering her ass with red heels places her hand with her red pointy nails flat on his chest, whispering in his ear.

I move to get up. "I think you're too busy to talk, Cesar." The girl looks at me with a sneer, but I ignore it.

"Who is she, Cesar? Why is she here?" She asks.

Cesar looks at me when he answers, "Someone very special to me." He removes her hand from his chest and looks at her. "Go wait for me outside." She doesn't argue and walks off.

"You're safe here with me, Rubi. You know I wouldn't let anything happen to you, and you can talk to me whenever you want. You know how things are here, so I need you to lock the door when I'm not here."

Great, another prison.

I scoff. "Let me know when I need the collar and the leash so you can walk me twice a day."

"It's not like that."

"Tell me, Cesar. What is it like?" I ask sarcastically. "I get to come out when you say it is okay to come out. I get to hear people fucking and getting high through the walls at night, making sure I lock the door to the room in case they mistake it for a free bed to fuck on. You take me to school and drop me off. Pick me from school and do it all over again for the next six months," I say dejectedly.

"I'm sorry."

It's not his fault. I know I'm being a bitch.

I slide my fingers in the strands of my hair near my scalp and let out a puff of air. "Look, I'm sorry. I don't mean to take it out on you."

He smirks. "My feelings aren't made of glass." He enters the room and closes the door, drowning out the noise. "And if it wasn't because I gave my word to Ky, I would be making you smile here." He leans close and lowers his lips near my ear. "After I make you come so hard, everyone would hear you screaming my name over the music."

A blush creeps up my cheek, and I rub my lips together, stifling a smile. Cesar has a way with words and is a huge flirt, but I can tell he means it.

"Not one to sugarcoat, are you?"

"Not my style, *Nena*."

"Who's the girl? She was about to claw my face."

He smiles, but it doesn't reach his eyes. "No one important." They never are. Not to him. He kisses my cheek. "If she touches you, I'll kill her."

Something heavy settles in my stomach because I know he would. This is different from Westlake Prep. This is the real world. A world I'm familiar with.

"Be careful."

"Always." He twists the doorknob, opening it and locking it

from the inside. "Make sure this door stays locked." I nod, and he walks out.

———

Halloween this year lands on a Friday. I've been getting curious stares at school for the past two weeks. The lockers are tagged with graffiti, but I'm relieved it doesn't say freak or some other dumb shit. The teachers here could care less if you pay attention or turn in your homework. A far cry from West Lake Prep.

Some guys I've seen at the house go to school here. All seniors. They sit together in class, at lunch, and everywhere they see fit. They run the school and the drugs that move in and out of it. I've stayed out of their way, and they stay out of mine.

Cesar gave me a new phone since I left the one Stephen gave me on the dining table the night I went with Ky. I've called Ky every day, but he responds with a text. Usually with, Are you okay? Do you need anything? Not with I miss you. I love you. Generic responses. Like a friend checking up on you.

I thought he was adjusting to the whole thing like I was, but when I called last night, and this morning, there was no text. No answer. I try not to think the worst, but it's hard not to with my luck and our history. Sometimes, I think I'm the luckiest person alive to have escaped jail time and the system. Then, everything around me turns to shit. Like I'm cursed or something.

I ran into the girl who looked at me like she wanted to claw me to death at lunch. The one that Cesar is screwing––Or one of them. From what I've heard, he screws most of the girls that visit the house. The walls are thin. Not that I care, but they don't like me. They think I'm the threat when I'm not.

I'm walking down the hall toward the student parking lot after the bell rings at the end of the day. Everyone is grabbing their stuff from their lockers and rushing out.

"Hey." I turn and find the girl with the claws giving me a warm smile.

I turn around and keep walking. "What do you want?"

"I wanted to know if you were going to the Halloween party at West Lake?"

"No. Why would why?" I ask, my curiosity peaked.

"Because some of us dress up and crash it. No one knows it's us, but since you went there, I figured..."

I stop and face her. "You figured what?"

She looks at her pointy red nails like they chipped, but they are perfect. Shiny and red. "I know I've given you dirty ass looks since you arrived, but I was jealous."

I arch a brow. "Jealous?" I ask curiously. "Of what?"

The girl is sex on legs. She has a pretty body and nails and turns heads everywhere she goes. She could wear whatever she wanted without worrying about looking like a monster.

"Of you."

I look at my old Converse sneakers and tattered jeans and then at her skinny jeans with a cute top showing an inch of her stomach. She has dark hair and arched eyebrows. Her lips are painted red, which should look over the top, but on her, it fits.

"You must be blind."

"I'm Katie, by the way," she rushes out. "I know your name is Rubi."

I roll my eyes. "What do you want, Katie?"

She chews on her bottom lip. "I want to get to know you."

She wants something. If she wanted to be my friend, she would have been nice to me since I arrived.

"You don't want to be my friend, Katie. So cut the shit."

She lets out a slow breath. "I see the way he looks at you."

I freeze, but then I remember she is talking about Cesar, not Ky.

"It's not what you think. Nothing is going on between us. Cesar is my friend. I've known him a long time."

She gives me a nervous smile. "So, it's true?"

I give her a confused look. "What are you talking about?"

"You and Ky."

"What do you know about Ky?"

"Enough."

123

"Like?"

My stomach clenches, and the scars on my back begin to itch for the first time in a long time. Enough means intimate, besides Ky running things here like a king.

"I didn't mean it like that. I mean... who doesn't. He isn't a monk."

I know that, but I don't want to be reminded of who he's been with when he doesn't answer my calls.

"Are you trying to gloat?"

Her eyes widen. "No!" She lets out a ragged breath. "Please, I'm not trying to fight with you or for you to hate me. I'm sorry we got off on the wrong foot. A couple of girls are heading out to the Halloween party tonight, and we wanted to know if you would come with us. No one has to know." She means Cesar. "Masks are required, so we are not recognized, but Ky will be there. I overhead Cesar talking to Ky last night."

Ky is going? That's why he wouldn't answer my calls.

"Alright, you have my attention, but I need to ask you something."

"Okay."

"Did you fuck Ky?"

I can see her throat when she swallows thickly. I know the answer, but I'm mentally preparing for what I'll find tonight. I want the truth.

"Yes."

I nod. "Who else in the house?" I ask darkly.

She looks away. "All of them." Her eyes find mine, and I see sadness. "Just like Cesar."

"What time should I be ready?"

"Eight. When it's dark enough. Cesar will be on a run. We will pick you up then." She motions to her hair. "The blonde girl named Sarah. She will be bringing the masks. We're all wearing black."

"Okay."

I'm about to turn and walk out. "Rubi?" I turn my head. "It didn't mean anything."

She means when she fucked Ky.

I rub my tongue over my keep front teeth, trying to keep my anger at bay. "It never does, Katie."

I walk to the student parking lot and see Cesar's black Charger by the curb.

"Is everything okay? You look like someone squashed your pet turtle."

Yeah, I'm peachy. I found out that all the girls inside the house I was staying at fucked the only person I loved. The one that said he loved me and to trust him. The one I took a beating for when I was ten years old. The one going to a Halloween party while I'm dying inside without him.

"I'm good," I lie, squeezing my book bag to my chest when he drives off.

I know what I will find tonight, but I need to know. I need to see if it's true. If he lied to me about loving me and it was all part of game.

I don't want to drive myself crazy fighting for someone who could never love me, waiting like an idiot for him to show up. I'm tired of living a lie since I was ten years old because I don't want to see the bigger picture. What has been staring right in front of me since I was born? I'm not wanted. And this was his plan to get rid of me.

CHAPTER FIFTEEN
Rubi

CONOR'S HOUSE is packed with people wearing costumes. The music is blaring, but the neighbors don't have a problem with it since it's Halloween on a Friday night. The streets are filled with kids trick-or-treating, knocking on houses for candy. It's one of my favorite holidays to celebrate, but I have a sinking feeling I will walk into a nightmare.

"Are you okay?" Katie asks, her voice muffled under her mask. Sarah brought us masks from the movie The Purge. Mine is white that reads KISS ME on the top in red letters.

"Yeah," I lie.

I'm nervous. There are so many people inside the house you can hardly walk. The entire school is here. Girls wear practically nothing despite the bite of cold air outside, but inside the house, it's hot. The smell of alcohol and sweat mixed with the smell of rubber from the mask on my face makes me want to gag.

We move through the throng of people, my eyes searching for Ky, but I don't see him.

People cheer toward the back, grabbing our attention. I follow Katie, Sarah, and two other girls that came along.

"Oh shit, the Purge is here!" One guy shouts. "We are all going to die! Yo... Ky!"

He points to us. "The Purge. Get the fuck up, man. They're coming after you," he jokes.

My head snaps up, hearing his name. The guy is obviously drunk of his ass already, with his hands raised and fingers pointed right at us.

My eyes search through the crowd. Katie stops in front of me, whipping around. "Go back!"

I shake my head. "No. Why?"

She shakes her head and looks like a killer from the movie. My stomach sinks from what I'm about to see.

"You shouldn't--"

"I need to."

I don't know her, and she doesn't know me, but I can tell it's something she wouldn't want to see if it was the other way around. I can respect that, but it's why I came.

"Are you sure?" I nod with my phone in hand, the camera app open.

She looks down at her feet for a few seconds and steps to the side.

My heart drops, and my hands begin to shake. I take a deep breath and grip the phone, steadily snapping pictures.

Ky is sitting on the couch. His face is painted black and white like the Day of the Dead. Shot glasses are lined on the coffee table. Jen is sitting on his lap with a lime in her mouth. She leans close, it slips, and she kisses him hard on the mouth. My heart is pounding. My knees are about to give out when he kisses her back. His hands slide to her waist, lifts her off, and stands unsteadily on his feet. Jen laughs, trying to wrap her arms around his neck, but he pushes her, shaking his head.

He steps forward, and Jen smiles, swaying into him. "You want to go upstairs?" She says with a sultry smile.

He's drunk, but there is no excuse. I want to scream at him. I want to fuck her up by wiping her with the floor, but that will never change what I saw. It would never undo the pain in my heart. I thought the worst thing in life was not having someone tell you they love you. But I was wrong. The worst thing is when they say the words, and it's a lie.

Ky might as well have been the one to beat with a belt, leaving me with the scars that will always remind me he was never mine. He never loved me. He was never my friend.

Anger bubbles up my throat. "Yeah, that's a great idea!" I shout.

Everyone's head turns.

"What are you doing?" Katie asks.

My eyes shift to hers. "What I do best. Survive."

"You see, even they think it's a great idea," Jen purrs with her hand around his waist in a tight black catsuit.

Ky looks up. His eyes are red from too much alcohol. When I pull off my mask and let my hair fall around my shoulders, Ky's face falls. He looks at Jen and then at me.

"Rubi?"

"Go ahead, Jen. He's all yours." She smiles triumphantly like that cat that got the cream.

He stumbles, attempting to push her away. "Rubi. No."

"You're right, Katie. It didn't mean anything."

"This is so fucked up," Katie says when I turn around.

"Is that..." Conor trails off dressed like a pimp, pointing at me from the right, but I keep walking toward the living room.

The music changes to some dance beat, muffling Ky screaming my name, "Rubiiiiii! Rubi... it's not what you think! Rubiiiii!"

Rushing out the door to the sidewalk toward the car, I slide into the backseat next to Katie, shutting the door. Ky stumbles out the front door, out of breath. The sound of tires screeching when a car breaks too hard has everyone freezing into place.

"What the hell?" Sarah says, pointing at the lifted truck that practically hit the car in the driveway. Tyler jumps out of his truck like a demon-possessed, walking inside the house without a costume, oblivious to what is happening. It looks like he is on a mission to unalive someone. I already messed up and showed my face. I'm not supposed to be here.

"Let's go," I tell Sarah.

"He's reeeeally messed up," Katie says, watching Ky trying to walk across the front lawn to the black Toyota Camry.

Surprisingly, he finds his balance and rushes to the car.

"R-Rubi, I... can explain. Pleease--"

"Go," I tell Sarah facing forward, not wanting to hear his bull-shit. She drives off, and I wince when I hear Ky screaming my name at the top of his lungs, his voice breaking. There is nothing to explain. It's black and white, and I proof in color.

I stare out the window at the kids going house to house, knocking on doors, and getting candy.

"What an asshole?" Katie says, shaking her head like I'm not here. "I can't believe....well, I can. But--"

"You're not making her feel better, Katie. That was fucked up. There really isn't much to say."

"I'm not trying to make her feel worse than she must be feel-ing, Loren. I wish someone could go kick his ass. You saw the look on her face."

"Shh...." I think that was Sarah.

The girl sitting next to me on my left is quiet. I don't know her name, but I feel her squeeze my hand, clenched into a tight fist on my lap. "My name is Paula," she says softly. "You deserve better."

Sounds like something Cesar would say. You deserve better. I look at the dark sky, finding the moon. Whenever I felt lost, I would see the moon because it was the only light when so much darkness surrounded me. The worst things that happened to me always happened at night.

My stepfather beat me after I came home from seeing Ky after it got dark. Watching my mother get high. My stepfather and his work buddies showed up before I went to bed to get high.

Mike.

The electricity getting shut off.

The pain in my stomach from hunger was always the worst at night. It felt like my body was feeding itself from inside. Nothing ever good happened to me when the sunset. It was like the demons were set free to take what they wanted because I was weak and held on to hope.

They say once you fall and hit the ground, there is no other way to go but up. It depends on how you stand, that will deter-mine how high you rise.

There is a loud knock on the bedroom door, but I drown it out. Just like the twenty text messages and fifteen missed calls from Ky on my phone for the past hour. I see the shadows of sneakers from the gap under the door from where I sit in the closet.

Another hard knock "Rubi?"

It's Cesar. He must have heard the news, or maybe Ky called him.

"Rubi, I know you're in the closet. Open the door, *Nena*. I need to make sure you're okay."

I grab the phone and send a text to his phone.

Rubi: I'm fine. I want to be left alone.

"He's sorry, Rubi. He said what you saw looked bad but didn't mean it. It's not what you think, Rubi. He was going to come, but I told him not to. I know you need time to think."

I look at the picture of Ky kissing Jen. Her annoying voice floated in my head. He always comes back to me. They must have gone to the party, and why he wasn't answering my calls. He thought I was stupid and wouldn't show up. That I would never find out.

I sent Cesar the picture. I hear the ping on his phone and a string of expletives coming from his mouth.

Rubi: I have nothing to say to him and don't want to ever see him again. Please, leave me alone.

He sighs, banging his fist on the door. "Rubi, I'm so sorry. You know I'm here for you, right? Always."

I don't answer, laying my head on the pillow I placed on the floor, looking at the picture from my phone screen, searing the image in my mind. A single tear slides down my cheek, closing my eyes, knowing the nightmares will come.

The smell of my mother's house.

The rough feel of the dirty carpet.

The sting from the leather on my skin.

The heat from the pain muffled my screams.

My stepfather's voice, *"Stupid little girl. I told you not to see that boy. No one wants you, but you don't listen."*

And he was right.

CHAPTER SIXTEEN
Ky

I KEEP CALLING, but she won't answer. Panic sets in. The cold feeling of dread every time she doesn't answer the phone or the texts, leaving them on read. My heart drops when my phone dings and her name floats on the screen.

I open the text and look at the picture. I bite the inside of my mouth, tasting blood, imagining what she must be feeling. What must be going through her head?

"Hey, man. Are you done throwing up?" Conor takes a pull from his beer. "You're going back inside, right?" Conor asks, dressed in his ridiculous pimp costume.

I threw up after drinking too much. I didn't mean to drink much, but I had so much on my mind, like how I could save her. How could I get rid of her father without her thinking I was an evil monster. Plus, I had to make it seem I wasn't with Rubi after she left. Stephen doesn't know where Rubi stays if she stays away and out of his life. But I want her in mine. Her showing up here was the worst thing that could have happened.

The music and laughter had my mind spinning. I felt numb. I couldn't get Jen's skinny ass off my lap and got sick when she kissed me. For one second, I thought I was in my room kissing Rubi. But the tongue and lips felt wrong. When I realized what was happening, I pushed Jen off me. Her spit was in my mouth, mixed with the taste of lime and tequila, turning my stomach. It felt wrong. Her taste... was all wrong.

"Hey." I look up, my eyes trying to focus on Jen walking toward me by the side of the house.

I point at her with disgust. "Get the fuck away from me," I snarl. "The shit you pulled earlier..."

"You never had a problem before."

She tries to arch her back slightly so her breast can spill from the neckline of the black suit she is wearing, doing nothing for my dick.

"Fuck off." I hock back and spit the sour taste from my mouth on the grass at her feet, making her flinch. I pressed my thumbs over my closed eyes, trying to calm myself down.

"You kissed me back."

I was in a drunk haze, and I swear I could feel her in the room. My thoughts went to Rubi like they have been since I was ten. Jen took advantage, knowing I was drunk.

I pushed Jen away, standing up, and my worst nightmare came alive. The look on Rubi's face broke me. It shattered me, and, in that moment, terror set in. I could feel her slipping from my fingers like a diamond falling into the deep ocean.

"I thought you were someone else. I'm sure you felt me pushing you off me. I don't think you're that dumb to figure out I'm not interested. I did come out here to throw up. I told you whatever we had was over."

She snorts. "I know we... aren't exclusive, but it never stopped you before."

I spit on the grass again. "Yeah, well, that was then, and this is now." I tilt my head up, looking at the dark sky, leaning on the side of the house.

I can feel her gaze studying me for a second, wishing she would just go away so I can think. I need to figure out how I will fix things with Rubi. I can't show up there acting like a fucking idiot pleading for forgiveness. I need to give her a day. One day is what I'll give her.

Jen steps forward, raising her hand toward my face. "You messed up the paint on your..."

I pull my face away out of her grasp, clenching my teeth.

"Don't touch me." I shake my head. "Why are you out here, huh? What part don't you get?"

She flinches. "What?"

"Get. The. Fuck...."

A piercing scream comes from inside the house over the beat of the music. I pause, thinking it's some Halloween prank. People start rushing out of the house.

"Oh my God, I don't think he's breathing!" Someone shouts.

"He beat the shit out of him!"

"Did you see his face?"

Fuck. A ball of dread weighs in my stomach. I run inside, trying to push through the bodies running out the front door. "Move!" I try to blink through the fog of the alcohol, trying to clear my head, pushing people out of the way in their stupid costumes, trying to find who they are talking about.

I look up the stairs. Girls are crying with their hands covering their faces. Makeup smeared. Face paint melting off like water-colors on a canvas.

When I reach the second floor, raised voices float from the bedroom. I see Conor placing his hands over his head, walking back and forth. "Fuck! What did you do?"

I push Conor out of the way, making my way inside. I blink, trying to take in the scene. Noah is naked on the floor with a sheet covering his lower half. His face turned to the side in a bloody mess. I look over and see the hostile look on Tyler's face. His jaw was tight, nostrils flaring, staring at Noah with split bloody knuckles.

Chris is kneeling on the floor, checking Noah's pulse. "Call 911!" He shouts. "I can hardly feel a pulse.

Conor is on his phone. My eyes swing toward the bed, and Abby is sobbing while clutching a sheet over her naked body. I look around the room for Abby's clothes, needing to calm her down before the paramedics come.

I find her clothes on the floor and hand them to her. "Abby, get dressed," I tell her softly.

Her eyes are red-rimmed, lips quivering, probably in shock, trying to wrap her head around what happened. "He...He.... W-wouldn't s-stop." Her eyes are full of tears, staring at Noah.

"Why? Why would you do that to him!" She cries. Tyler turns his head with a blank expression, stepping toward her. "You had no right, Tyler! Get away. Get away from me!" She cries.

"Get dressed, Abby. They will be here any minute." That is all I can say. I wish I could tell her I could take her to the hospital, but I'm not fit to drive.

Conor is talking to the dispatcher on the phone. His eyes find mine. "They will be here in two minutes. They say not to move him." He nods his chin toward Abby. "She's been screaming. A lot."

Chris looks up at me. "He's going to go to jail, Ky." He looks at Noah. "Fuck, man....hang in there, Noah."

Abby gets dressed and rushes to Noah, kneeling by his side, afraid to touch him. "Noah." Tears run down her cheeks. "P-Please, Noah. Please, be okay." She looks around the room for his clothes and grabs them, trying to get his boxers and handing them to Chris.

Tyler pushes off the wall. She panics with a look of terror when she rushes behind me. "Ky, get him away from me."

Tyler shakes his head with his hands up with a torn expression, "Abby, I would never hurt you. I'm sorry. You have to believe me...I didn't mean..."

"What the fuck, Tyler? Why?" I ask.

But I know why. I understand why he did it, and I must admit, if it was Rubi and another guy I walked in on, I would have lost it, too. Look what I did to Chris's car for taking Rubi out to the movies. I know that sounds fucked up because Noah is a good guy, and I'm no saint, but you can't help who you love. Even if you try to convince yourself otherwise by using others to cover up the truth.

Noah likes Abby more than I thought he did. But, in Tyler's case, he pushed Abby away, and she obviously moved on.

He grips his hair, pulling it from his scalp. "I'm sorry, Abby. I fucked up. I'm so sorry. I..."

The paramedics rush in, working on Noah. Then the cops show up.

Conor talks with them in hushed tones.

Two police officers turn their heads and step farther into the room. "Tyler Murray?" Tyler turns around. "Hands behind your back."

Tyler turns, placing his hands behind his back. The sound of handcuffs being placed on his wrist. He looks behind me. "I'm sorry, Abby. You're my..."

"You had no right," she says, her voice breaking.

Tyler hangs his head. "Ky, call my father." And they hall him away.

A female officer walks in after they take Noah on a stretcher. "We will need a statement from her about what happened and anyone who saw anything."

"She can give you one at the hospital," Chris says.

I fish out my keys to my car, looking at Abby. I ask, "Can you drive?" She nods. "Let's go." I look at Chris. "I'll make the call on the way to the hospital. Call Noah's parents."

Abby pulled away from the curb, heading to the hospital after I called Tyler's father, letting him know what happened, and they took Tyler to jail. I send a text letting my father know what is happening, and then Cesar, for the second time tonight. First, I asked him about Rubi and said that I was sorry and that it wasn't what it looked like. I also scolded him for letting Rubi out of his sight and let him know about Tyler.

"Why?" Abby sniffs.

"You know why," I reply quietly.

"He kept hitting him...and hitting him," she cries on a snob staring out the windshield.

Chris leans forward, his hand on the side of my seat. "Noah is a tough kid, Abby. He was breathing, and they were able to stabilize him. I'm not going to give you shit about finding you with Noah. Everything is going to be okay."

I look over my shoulder. "You know what this means for Tyler, right?"

Chris sighs. "Yeah, jail time. He can kiss college goodbye. He probably won't graduate-- Not this year. Football is fucked. And you know what? He deserves it. All we can hope for is that Noah is okay and can fully recover."

"Things are going to get out of hand, and when they find out Tyler trains at the dojo, it won't help him in his case. But we need to do one thing at a time. I agree. We need to if Noah pulls through, and then we will worry about Tyler. We can bond him out." I look at Abby. "Tell them what happened, Abby. It's obvious, but don't make Tyler out to be this monster."

"But..."

"He fucked up, Abby. We all know what he did. It's bad. But he's not a monster. I'm not excusing what he did, but you have to understand he is like a brother to us. He's one of us."

I don't tell her how all this puts Rubi at risk.

"He won't be bothering you, Abby. Ever. I'll make sure of it," Chris adds.

CHAPTER SEVENTEEN
Ky

AFTER THE SHIT show in the waiting room with Noah's parents shouting at Stephen and Caroline, promising to lock their son up for good, I sit in my car listening to my father on the Bluetooth from my car.

"You know what this means, Ky. This puts Rubi in more danger, with Tyler in jail. I spoke to the lawyers. Tyler is looking at assault and battery. I'm sure Noah's parents will press charges. Stephen already called, and they will provide Noah the best care."

"He has a broken jaw, nose, and eye socket, they said. He also has a concussion, but he's stable." I blow a puff of air. "How long?"

He knows I'm asking how long Tyler will likely be in jail.

"I can get him bonded out for the time being, but he will serve time as an adult. This isn't going to be pushed under the rug. His parents have money, and they have good lawyers. He won't be graduating this year, and he will lose his scholarship, most likely be repeating his senior year, and Chris's father wants a restraining order so he won't be able to get near Abby."

"What about Rubi?"

She is all I care about. All I can think about. No one gives a shit about her, but I do. Tyler feels guilty, but I didn't see him putting up much of a fight when her father wanted her gone.

"She is in more danger. Tyler is looking at assault and battery. Noah's parents claim that Tyler has threatened Noah before. It doesn't look good. The board will see that he is not fit and unstable, which puts Stephen's plan on hold, which also means Rubi's existence is a bigger problem, and I can't use my connections in this situation. It will draw too much attention to other business."

"So now what?"

"If Stephen cannot get the board to agree to his son taking over his portion of things, he will get rid of Rubi to ensure it happens because he would be the only living heir."

My blood turns cold.

"Define getting rid of Rubi."

"He's going to kill her, Ky."

A maniacal laugh escapes my throat, imagining the look on Stephen's face when I kill him. "You know that isn't going to happen."

"You can't get involved, Ky," he says, raising his voice.

I turn down the volume. My heart thuds in my chest as sinister thoughts filter into my mind of how I can make Stephen disappear.

"So he can do whatever he wants..."

"She isn't important to anyone in our circle that makes decisions."

I clench my teeth. "She's important to me."

"I know, son, but it is what it is. You have her."

"But I can't protect her, Dad. I need to make sure nothing happens to her. If you can't back me on this..."

"I can't, and you cannot get involved. There is too much at stake."

A sinking feeling forms in my stomach, imagining Rubi hurt.

"I don't care about any of it, and you know it. Don't make me defy you. For Rubi, I will, and you know it. If something happens to her..."

"Make sure she stays where she is. She can't pop up at the house, Ky...at school, or anywhere... It will get back to him. She is a loose end in his life that he thought would never come back to haunt him."

"Did he know--about Rubi?"

I want the truth.

"Initially, no. They contacted him after her mother died. He knew then."

"And he didn't..."

"He mentioned it to me, and I told him to sort it."

I snort. "By abandoning her and leaving in foster care, that's sorting it."

"He thought it would go away by ignoring it, and no one would find out, but when the board started pulling out conditions on who could take over the company. He started to worry because she is technically older than Tyler."

"But Rubi was born out of wedlock."

My father sighs. "Doesn't matter, not in the state of Georgia."

"What does that mean?"

"She gets equal shares to everything even if she is illegitimate, and if he dies, she is entitled to equal shares. All she has to do is prove that she is his daughter, and it's not too difficult since she was put through the system. I'm sure her mother knew she was a meal ticket waiting for the right time to show up and demand what was rightfully hers. It is probably why she moved so close to Stephen."

Something is not adding up. Rubi's mother knew where her father was the whole time but was too stressed to do anything about it. After finding out what Rubi's stepfather did to her because of me, I always wondered why. What was the big deal?

A nagging feeling crawls up my spine. Did they know? Are they afraid that Rubi would find out and be taken away by Stephen before time?

"Did Stephen ever tell you what happened to her stepfather?"

"Why are you asking?" My father asks. The sound of his leather chair groaning in the background. He's probably nursing a scotch in one of his many offices somewhere. I keep looking toward the exit doors of the emergency room department every time they slide open, waiting for Chris to walk out.

"I need to ask him a couple of questions. He's next on my list of loose ends."

"Ky," my father warns.

"Don't tell me to stop because that will only make me want to do it without getting the answers I need."

"Son, do you really love Rubi?"

"You know the answer. It is not hard to figure out."

"Does she know you? The real you, Ky. The things you have done and what you will do?"

She knows the real me. The parts of me that no one does. She knows my favorite color. My dreams. Dreams I haven't shared with anyone, but there are things Rubi doesn't know about the things I have done that have shaped who I am now.

I have given her an idea, but she needs to learn the truth. That is the part that scares me the most. I will lose her if I haven't lost her already with my stupidity. I should have never gone to the party, but I needed everyone to see that she wasn't part of my life. She is my life.

"I was getting there, but..."

"You need to play this smart Ky. This is dangerous, and you know it. Stephen has made a name for himself. Remember, he is a player and keeps his mouth shut. If your grandfather gets wind of you meddling, he will come for you, Ky, and there is nothing you can do about it. You will be on the next flight to Italy, taking your rightful place. And where will that leave Rubi?"

He is right, but I don't want to think the worst. I need her to trust me, and right now, I'm in the fucking doghouse. The thought of Cesar in the next room from where she sleeps drives me insane. Holding her after a nightmare or carrying her from the closet to the bed.

"Alright, but I'm not leaving her. Ever."

I hang up, knowing it's going to piss him off, but I need to dial Cesar again.

After the third ring, he picks up. "Yeah."

"Where is she?"

"Holed up in her room. She doesn't want to talk. Not even to me." I'm relieved but worried all at the same time. "Your right. Give her a day."

That is the same as torture.

She won't answer, and I'm sure she won't tomorrow or the next day, but I need to see her.

"I need to see her. Something happened..." Chris walks out and spots my car. "I'll tell you when I get there."

"Alright."

He hangs up at the same time Chris slides in the passenger seat.

"What's the update on Noah?" I ask.

"Tyler almost killed him, but he's alive."

"But he didn't, and that is all that matters."

Tyler is not a bad guy, and I can even call him one of my best friends, but if I had to choose between him and Rubi. It will always be Rubi.

Chris lets out a sigh in frustration. "I want to kick his ass, Ky. Did you know?"

I play dumb. "About?"

"Him and my sister."

"No," I lie. "I had no idea."

Tyler has been fighting his feelings for Abby since I caught them together in the pool. I don't know if he's slept with her or how far he's gone with Abby, but it's obvious this is more than a simple crush. He caught Noah fucking her in the bedroom and lost his fucking mind.

"I should be mad at Noah, but I'm not. Abby is old enough to make her own decisions, and she has never discouraged me when..." he trails off.

I want to punch him in the throat and bash his fucking head in. But I take a deep breath.

"It could be worse....I mean... if it was you, I found with...who I think you are talking about. I wouldn't be at a hospital waiting to see if you were okay." I smile.

He swallows nervously, but his face is tight. "What do you mean?"

He has some backbone. I give him that.

"If I walked in on you fucking Rubi, I would be waiting

outside while they tried to identify your body parts. Your parents wouldn't be able to bury what was left."

"You're fucking crazy."

"I think that has been established, but that didn't stop you."

"I thought a girl like Jen was more your style."

I roll my eyes. "I like the nice guy act you try to pull off. Thinking that will convince Rubi you are nothing like me. It's not like you didn't fuck Jen or her friends."

I watch him squirm in his seat. Chris hates it when I point out the truth.

"Why? Are you jealous I did? Is that why you fucked up my car because I can have her and Rubi if I wanted?"

Okay, he does have balls. Let's see how big. I place the car in drive and pull out of the parking lot onto the road.

The air is thick between us, and I know he feels it, too. He fidgets when he sees that I'm driving out of our neighborhood.

After a few minutes, the tension builds as I drive in silence, taking a turn toward the abandoned warehouses. Graffiti is everywhere. Garbage and broken glass bottles are strewn in the streets. No cars. There isn't a soul in sight, and the deeper I drive, the darker it gets.

"Why are we here?" Chris asks, looking around.

He's cagey. Afraid even.

Chris thinks he is safe from me because our fathers are business partners. I admit that would have been the case before Rubi showed up. Now that she is here and back in my life, things have changed. They have shifted.

"You said I was jealous of you. There is a big difference between jealousy and protecting what is mine."

"What does that have to do with you bringing me here?"

I turn my head, looking straight at him. "Everything, Chris. This is the part where I show you the lengths I'm prepared to go to to protect what is mine. What I own. What belongs to me."

"What belongs to you, Ky?" He mocks.

"Rubi. She belongs to me. The others, you could have a

fucking orgy, and I wouldn't give a fuck. You can spill cum down their throats for all I care, but Rubi" ––I grin–– "Rubi is mine."

"You're crazier than I thought. She isn't here. Her father sent her away like Tyler said."

I laugh, shaking my head at his stupidity for believing the bullshit Stephen came up with when he thought my father was handling things for his benefit.

I pull out my Glock from the waist of my jeans and chamber a round.

"What the fuck are you doing?"

"What does it look like? I'm protecting what is mine. When someone tries to touch something that belongs to you with the intent of stealing it, you kill him. Like an intruder, you're standing your ground. It's simple." I aim the gun at his head. "So...how do you want to die? Slow? Quick?"

He tries to open the door, but I flick the lock every time he reaches for it. "What the fuck, Ky?"

Pussy.

"Answer the question"––I wave the gun––"How do you wanna die?"

His eyes widen. His breathing quickens. He's scared. Terrified.

"I-I'm sorry, alright," he sputters. "It wasn't like Rubi was your girlfriend. To be honest, you've never had a girlfriend. Ever. I know for a fact you didn't sleep with her, so I took a shot. I'm a guy. She's gorgeous."

"Are you sure about that?"

His mouth turns into a frown. "There's no way. You hated her most of the time she was at school. You said..."

"It's none of your business, but I slept with her, Chris. In my bed. All night, licking her scars."

He knows I don't take girls into my room, and I'm staking my claim. He has two options: he backs off and lives–– or dies. I'm extending the courtesy because he is part of the future due to our father's business partnership.

"Then why the games, Ky? You want her so bad that you are willing to kill anyone who looks at her, but your tongue was down Jen's throat a while ago at a party where Rubi showed up. I'm sure everyone saw how important she is to you. Now you are waving your gun in my face, gloating. Threatening me?" He scoffs. "Take me home, Ky."

I grip the gun, my knuckles turning white, hating the fact that he's right.

Kissing Jen wasn't supposed to happen. I can't tell him the truth. I need to make it seem that way so her father won't go after her. The truth is, I'm terrified that she would never look at me the same way again. That she will think she means nothing to me.

I lower the gun, clear the round, and then hook it back into my jeans. "You don't understand," I tell him, pulling the car around to drop him off at his house.

"Look, I don't know what is going on between Rubi and her situation with her father...or what you two have going on, but I'll back off Rubi. If she means that much to you. I think you fucking up my car was enough."

"You took her out on a date."

"I did."

"I've never taken her out on a date. Not a formal one," I admit.

"What's stopping you?"

"It's complicated, but I think I messed things up with her."

"You did." He sighs and continues, "You were drinking and Jen has a way of sliding in to test the waters. She likes the attention she gets, and she was going out of her fucking mind when you started paying attention to Rubi, but you can't pull out a gun every time a guy looks at her, Ky."

I change the subject. "What are you going to do about Tyler?"

He sneers. "I want to kick his ass for thinking he had a chance with my sister and going behind my back. It was fucked up what he did to Noah."

"Is she okay?"

He shakes his head. "She's terrified of Tyler and wants nothing to do with him." He half shrugs. "I think Abby really felt something for Noah."

"Not to disrespect Abby, but she was fucking him."

He snorts. "Dude, I don't want to hear that about my sister. It's cringy as fuck."

"It's true. Little Abby is growing up. She is not little anymore, and now the whole school, including your parents, knows what she was doing when Tyler lost his fucking mind."

"Tell me about it. My father asked what the fuck was I doing, not watching her. He is mad about the whole thing. I'm probably grounded for the rest of the year, and Abby is no longer allowed to go out."

I smirk. "What were you doing?"

"You don't want to know."

"Probably the same thing."

"Something like that." He pulls a slasher mask from his pocket. The latex kind that folds. "Nicole wanted to suck me off wearing this."

I chuckle. "I guess I don't have to worry about you touching my girl."

"Like I said, I got the picture when you fucked up my car and threatened to kill me."

"I'm sorry about the car but not about the threat."

"Fair enough, but I'm not a pussy."

"That is still up for debate, asshole. You were fucking scared when I pulled my gun out, asking you how you wanted to die."

"I wasn't scared."

I turn my head. "You were. You almost ran out of the car," I laugh.

"Fuck you, man," he says, shoving me playfully. "I thought I was your friend."

"You are. If not, you would be dead in a ditch somewhere. Now, you know."

He runs his fingers through his hair. "I get it. Rubi is off-limits. It's not like she is around anyway, so at least you don't have to worry about guys at school hitting on her."

If he only knew it's not the guys I'm afraid of. It's if...she would speak to me after what happened.

CHAPTER EIGHTEEN
Ky

"WHAT'S UP?" Cesar says when I walk in the house after dropping off Chris.

"Has she come out?"

He shakes his head with a worried expression. "Nah. She is still in her room."

Katie and Sarah are sitting next to three other girls on the couch on their phones.

I nudge my head in their direction and ask, "Why were they there?"

"It wasn't my idea. They waited until I left to go on a run after you came back."

I didn't answer Rubi's calls because I was handling an incoming shipment from overseas on the coast. The guys started teasing me about Rubi after I turned down every girl who asked me to go with them to the Halloween party. I figured that was my chance.

I step closer into the living room, ignoring the other guys that run in Cesar's crew sitting on the loveseat. Katie is the first to look up, a worried expression crossing her features. "What the fuck were you five trying to pull going to a West Lake prep party with Rubi?"

All five girls look up. All seniors that attend West Park with Rubi. I'm not an idiot. They want an in, and they thought Rubi was it.

"We didn't force her. She wanted to go," Katie says defensively.

Of course, she did. I wasn't answering, and she wanted to see if I would be there. It was a test, and I failed miserably.

"Do you know what you've done?"

Sarah has the balls to roll her eyes at me and her next words slap my face. "What? It's not our fault. How did we know you would be there doing what you do best. It's not like it was a surprise. We have all been there-- under you."

Guilt eats me from the inside. I want to barge into the room, pull Rubi from the closet, and hold her. I want to tell her that I love her, but how. I have slept with every girl sitting in this room and I'm sure she knows it. It's not a secret. Sarah just threw it in my face. But being the proud asshole that I am. I won't show her how ashamed I am.

"It's obvious you weren't memorable. To be honest, I hardly know any of your names. If I hear you take Rubi anywhere like that again, I will drag your ass out of here and make you disappear."

I get up and head down the hallway, not caring if her door is locked, and she refuses to talk to anyone. I need to see her. I need to tell her about Tyler.

"It's four in the morning," Cesar says.

"I can tell time." I stand in front of her door, about to pick the lock.

He leans on the wall. "You think that's a good idea?"

"I need to see her. We need to talk."

He snorts. "Good luck."

I'm going to need it.

After I pick the lock, I open the door, not bothering to look at the bed or call out her name, heading for the closet.

I slide the doors open slowly, feeling like my heart is lodged in my throat, beating like a jackhammer. I see her sleeping form lying on the floor with the comforter under her, watching her shiver, and I fall in love with her all over again...like the first time I saw her all those years ago.

"What are you doing up there?" A girl is trying to jump over the wood fence by the tall hedges in my backyard. Her long, straight

hair blows in the breeze. The sun glittering on a couple of strands, making it look shiny. She looks like an angel that came from the sky.

"Hi." She jumps down with a thud when her shoes touch the freshly cut grass. Her sneakers look old, like the ones you see in the donations box at the sneaker store to recycle worn shoes. "My name is Rubi," she says, wiping her hands on her pants. "I didn't know there were big houses on this side."

"There is," I reply, watching her fidget with the end of her shirt. It's faded and looks like it's old. Little pink hearts are peeling off, and her jeans look worn and two sizes too big, but her face reminds me of an angel. Like the ones you see in a church.

She rubs her lips together like she's scared I'll tell her to leave. But then I remembered I didn't tell her my name.

"My name is Ky."

She smiles, and my stomach feels funny, like when my mom used to push me on the swing at the park, and I get those tiny little flutters.

"Do you want to play a game?"

She looks around, and I realize that sounds stupid because what could we play in the backyard when all my outdoor stuff is inside the house.

She watches the daisies sway in the wind by the hedges near the big tree. "Those flowers are pretty."

I never thought of flowers being pretty, but maybe that's because I'm a boy and not supposed to. But I agree anyway.

"They are." I almost say not as pretty as she is, but that would sound weird, and the last thing I wanted her to think was--that I was weird.

She plucks two flowers and steps closer with a bright smile. "We each take turns pulling a petal and whoever ends with the last petal has to answer a question."

I've heard of this game at school during recess. You pull the petals on the chance to see if a boy loves you or not. Some girls at the playground do it with any flower they can find. The daisies are in the backyard because they were my mother's favorite, and she had the gardener plant them. I used to hate them after she left. I hated everything that had to do with my mother. I didn't care what she used to do or what she liked; she didn't care about me. I almost pulled them out, but I'm glad I didn't.

She walks a few steps and sits in front of me on the grass, and I do the same, with our knees almost touching.

She held the flower by the stem toward me, and I promised myself she would never have to wonder if I loved her. She would never have to play the game to find out because the answer would always be the same. I love her, and I think I always will.

I gently carry her to the bed, ensuring I don't wake her. I pick up the pillow, placing it under her head. I pull the comforter over her. I remove my pants and shirt, leaving my boxers on, glad I washed the face paint off at the hospital.

I flick the lock on the bedroom door and slide in next to her, making sure I keep her warm, holding her tight against my chest. I hope that when she wakes up, she will give me the chance to explain. I fall asleep to the smell of her hair and the softness of her skin.

CHAPTER NINETEEN
Rubi

MY EYES POP OPEN, the feeling of something warm and heavy enveloping me. For a second, I thought I was back in my father's house when Ky would carry me to bed every night. I hear voices coming from the other side of the wall and realize I'm in the house with Cesar. I shift and feel something warm and heavy behind me. I look at the closet doors wondering how I got into the bed. I freeze.

"Go back to sleep, *principessa.*"

Memories of last night coming in full force and the pain starts all over again. My heart shattering into a million pieces. The hours spent crying. How alone I felt. Now he's here. Telling me to go back to sleep like nothing happened.

I sit up and he pulls me right back down pinning me to bed with my arms over my head.

"What the hell, Ky?"

He pins me with a stare hating how gorgeous he is. How he makes me feel.

"I need to talk to you."

"Send a text."

"Not that simple."

My lips curls into a sneer. "It is. You manage to use your mouth and your dick, I'm sure you could figure it out."

He grins. "You want me to show you how I manage to do all three?"

He presses his morning wood against my thigh. My nose flairs trying to ignore the tingling between legs.

161

"No thanks. Go ask Jen, or you can simply walk outside the room. I'm sure you can go down memory lane with some of the girls you have fucked."

"I don't want them."

I try to wiggle my hands free but his grip tightens on my wrists. "I need to talk to you. Something happened last night..."

"A lot of the things happened last night."

"It's not about that and for the record, I didn't sleep with her... or anyone. Not since you." His eyes trail stopping at the v of my black t-shirt reminding me that I'm not wearing a bra and my nipples are hard, but I'm not falling for it.

When his eyes meet mine again there is something I haven't seen since we were kids. Tenderness. Need. But not the kind of need that requires sex. It's the kind that needs to re-connect. The kind where two people meet and fall for each other.

"It's Tyler."

Something happened. If he is here, it has something to do with me.

"What about him?"

"He's in jail, Rubi."

Oh my God! Tyler in jail means something bad happened.

I squirm. "Let me up, Ky."

He releases me and I sit up drawing my knees to my chest. "What happened?"

"It's Noah."

My eyes must look puffy and red rimmed because I close my eyes feeling the sting from crying. A cold feeling settles in my chest.

"What happened to Noah?"

"He's in the hospital," I nod and he tells me everything in detail.

My thoughts go to Abby and what she must be feeling. Torn between a boy she gave her heart to and broke it, and the one she gave the pieces to promising to fix it.

I get up and walk to the ensuite bathroom. Cesar insisted on me taking this room for privacy and I couldn't be more grateful.

"You need to listen to me," Ky says watching me brush my teeth. "You need to be careful."

"From what? You."

"I'm the least of your worries. You don't have to be scared of me, Rubi."

I'm terrified of him. It feels like my whole life has revolved around him and only him. The innocence of first love in a young girl's heart can be magnified times a hundred because she didn't receive it at home, holding on to the first person that gave it. It didn't matter that it was the right or wrong kind––the toxic kind. Anything was better than what I was raised with. It was something to hold on to but now I'm terrified because love hurts. Sometimes I think it hurts more to love than to never have experienced it.

"You have to be careful where you go because Tyler will do time in jail for what he did to Noah and that puts you in danger with Stephen."

"You don't know that."

"I spoke to my father and he has the best lawyers. Noah's parents have pressed charges and Abby's parents want a restraining order. Like I said, Tyler is in jail and he will do time for what he did. Noah will make a full recovery but it will be a long one. He's banged up pretty bad."

My chest squeezes. "Poor Noah. He didn't ask for this."

"Tyler is remorseful. He just...lost control. And now he has to the pay the price. He was the aggressor and he threatened Noah. The judge is not going to excuse what he did that easily."

I know he's right but what does that have to do with me?

"How does that involve me exactly?"

"Stephen doesn't want you to inherit. You're the oldest, Rubi. If Tyler is in jail and tried for what he has done, it makes your juvenile charges look like child's play in comparison. Literally."

I feel like I've been punched in the stomach. The scars on my back tingle like they did when they were trying to heal. "Is that the only reason he wanted me gone?"

"It's why he popped up to begin with. He planned on getting

you to sign away your rights but when he found out that we were getting close, he got nervous."

I take a seat on the edge of the bed trying to make sense of it. "If I didn't know about him to begin with, I wouldn't have known. So why did he show up?"

"The court and social services would have told you about him and one day you might want to contact him and he didn't want to take the chance in you finding out. It doesn't matter if it was now or later, you're entitled to an equal share of his fortune, Rubi. If the board see's that you are fit to run his portion of the company in his place, you can take control over Caroline and Tyler."

"I'm not familiar with laws but doesn't he have to die for me to inherit anything anyway?"

He snorts "Not necessarily. When he retires or the board wants a change because they feel he is burned out, they look for the next one in line. The plan was for Tyler, Chris, and me to take over the business when the time comes but that has changed. Stephen...he... doesn't want you, Rubi."

I blink away the tears. "I'll sign whatever he wants but I don't want to see him ever again. I'll change my name. I'll move as far away as I can but I don't want to see him."

"I wish I could say it was simple as signing a piece of paper but the board will get involved and his share of the company would be at stake. Caroline suffers mental depression so she is out, but you. Your record has been expunged since it was an offense committed before you turned eighteen. You're clean, Rubi."

I pinch my brows together. "How?"

"I made it go away. My father called whoever he needed to call. It's done, but that makes you a target now and I'm sorry. I'm sorry that you have shitty parents and that they failed you." Tears run down my cheeks and he swipes them away with his thumb. "Don't cry." He wraps his arms around me but I pull away.

How can I not cry. Everyone in my life has failed me. They've hurt me. Pushed me away. Now my father wants to kill me.

"What now?"

"I protect you." He holds my face in his hands. "He will come after you, Rubi. I can promise you that."

"Who are you people, huh?"

He pulls the sleeve of his black shirt revealing the tattoo with the stars. The one he said meant loyalty. "This is given to heirs of the Italian mafia passed down to children and their children for generations. I'm not supposed to be here. I was never supposed to be born in the U.S."

"You're in the Italian mafia?"

"I come from a dangerous family. My father wanted to give me a choice because of my mother. She didn't like my father's obligation so he created his own legacy here but he couldn't cut ties." He leans in close. "You see, Rubi. They don't know that. They think my father runs some drugs and I play gangster with Cesar but that is just a smoke screen. I can protect you. Please, let me."

"I don't know." And that's the truth. "I need time to think. I-I need space."

He flinches like I struck him but I'm not sure about anything anymore. All I know is that I want to finish high school. It's the only thing I have going for me. I want to live. I want to be happy.

He wants to protect me because he thinks Stephen is going to wipe me off the face of the earth, fine. But that is where it ends.

"Alright. I'll back off but I'm going to be around... a lot. There will be people looking out for you for protection."

"Fine, but we are friends. That's it."

He licks his bottom getting up. "Get dressed."

"Why?"

"I'm taking you out for breakfast."

"No."

"Then, I'll stay here and watch you."

"That's creepy."

"Get dressed then."

CHAPTER TWENTY
Rubi

"YOU SURVIVED." I turn to find Katie behind me, walking inside the main entrance.

"I did. He wouldn't leave, and it's not like I can kick him out."

"He does own the place."

I figured, and I'm not surprised.

"I'm sorry."

"For what?" I stop at my locker, noticing something new written on it. It reads Ky loves Rubi.

"Is this for real?"

"He has his ways, I'm sure."

"I told him I needed space."

"Ouch. You haven't forgiven him, then. There is a bet, you know."

I close my locker. "A bet?"

She scrunches her nose. "Yeah, me, Sarah, and the other girls––the guys too. Half said you would take him back, and the other half said no. It's a three-hundred-dollar pot."

"We weren't together, so the bet is null and void. You guys should quit and get your money back." I pause, wondering if she could help me. "Katie?"

"Yeah?"

"Do you know where I could get a job?"

"A job?"

"Yeah, I need the money. It's not like I live with mom and dad."

"You live in a house where money isn't a problem."

"It's not my money; I won't ask for it. It's bad enough Cesar has been buying me food and taking me to school."

"I get it. I'll come up with something."

"Thanks, Katie." Her eyes widen, looking behind me. "What?"

I see a tall guy with dark hair and brown eyes the color of honey walking through the halls, watching every girl give him a once-over as he passes.

"He's here."

"Who?"

"Manny. He's a tattoo artist. He moved here from Ohio and is one of Cesar's close friends. They're boys."

"Oh, I've never seen him before."

She grins and says softly so he can't hear. "Trust me, now that you have, it's hard to forget."

My eyes follow him, noticing the ink on his arms and how every one of Cesar's friends pay him attention like he's famous. When his eyes land on mine, I look away, hoping he doesn't think I am staring.

He's nice looking, but I was looking at his ink.

"He's coming over here," she mumbles.

Manny walks up to us, his honey-brown eyes meeting mine. "Hey, Katie." He greets her with a kiss on the cheek.

"Hi," she replies, but he keeps staring at me.

"Who's your friend?" He asks.

"This is Rubi. She transferred from West Lake Prep."

"Hi, I'm Manny," he says, holding his hand out for a hand-shake. I shake it. "What brings you to the dark side?"

I pull my hand, rubbing it where he touched me. "I grew up here––"

"Then you hit the jackpot," he teases with a glint in his eye. "Must have been hard coming back."

I watch Katie wince from the corner of my eye. I'm sure Cesar told her how we know each other. "Not exactly," I reply.

His eyes take in my designer hoodie and ripped jeans. "How come?"

He's judging me. I'm unsure if I should be upset, but he doesn't know me, and I shouldn't care less what he thinks.

"Because I'm from here."

He snorts. "Okay, nice sweater, by the way." He gives Katie a hug, dismissing me. "I'll see you later beautiful. I gotta get to class."

"Okay," she says, then he walks away.

"I'm sorry about Manny. I've never seen him be so rude to a girl before. He is usually not..."

"A judgmental prick."

"He was an ass, but that is because he doesn't know you."

She doesn't either, but I don't want to be a bitch pointing it out. Katie knows a lot of people, and I need her to get me a job.

In class, I look at my sweater Manny pointed out. Manny was trying to say that I don't fit in here wearing it, but he doesn't know I don't have options. I hardly have any clothes besides what Ky stuffed in my closet. Hence, why I need a job. It is still warm enough to wear tank tops. I should stop hiding in my sweaters. Hiding who I am. Hiding what my stepfather did to me.

I could cover up the tattoo with Ky's name like I planned but was thwarted by him showing up. There are a lot of things that need to change in my life, but I need to start with myself.

After Cesar drops me off at the house from school, I shower and change, heading to the kitchen and noticing the pile of dishes the guys leave after they hang out.

I tie my long hair in a messy bun, not caring that the scars on my back are visible. I do not care what anyone thinks when they see the monster I look like underneath. I'm tired of being judged. I'm tired of hiding and caring what people will say about me.

I find the cleaning supplies and get to work before everyone arrives, usually around five or so. I can hear some of the guys laughing outside, but I ignore it, opting for the corded headphones that came with my cell phone. I tap the music app on my phone and surprised I have a subscription knowing it was Ky.

I haven't forgiven him for him kissing Jen at the party. It wasn't like we were in a serious relationship, but for a second, I thought we were. I thought it meant more like I always did when it involved Ky. Maybe he agreed to sleep with me because of Cesar, and it was a territorial thing. It's my fault because I was the one who came on to him. I was using Cesar as an excuse, but now I know better.

My thoughts go to the morning in the shower, where he stopped me from pleasuring him. He said it wasn't about having sex. I believed him. He said he loved me the night before. I felt like I owed him a part of me that I never gave him. My body. But something was holding me back from saying those words in return. Trust. I didn't trust him. Not with that part of me. And I was right not to.

I scrub the plate, letting the water rinse the soap off, wondering when it would stop. The hate for my existence.

Once again, I was snared in a web by those three little words I was desperate to hear from someone all my life. I hate myself for believing the first person that said them. It takes me back to the scared little girl I was, hoping the pain was worth it. Every mark on my back turned into another scar. Every tear shed, hoping it was worth it.

It was all for nothing.

The scars.

The tears.

The pain.

It didn't matter. It all ended in heartbreak, landing back to where I started. Alone.

After I wash the dishes, I start on the floors. The front door swings open, and a couple of the guys walk in, sidestepping the part where I just mopped, giving me a small grin.

When I continued, I could feel their eyes on my back like the heat from the burning sun. I try not to look at the expressions of disgust and horror. I did this to myself, and I'm owning it.

Cesar walks in, and everyone shifts on the sofa. His eyes narrow at everyone behind me, and then his eyes soften when they land on me with the wooden mop in my hands. I pull the cord from the headphones. "Why are you cleaning, *Nena*?"

I look around at the dirty coffee table I still need to clean and the areas where the guys sit. "I thought I could help out. This place was a mess and..."

"You don't have to do that." His eyes notice the black cami I'm wearing, exposing my shoulders and back. His eyes shift to the guys and then back to me.

I shrug my shoulders, my eyes pleading with him to not make a big deal. "Ky..."

My jaw hardens. "I don't care what Ky thinks or does. He isn't my keeper."

He raises his brows in surprise. He thought I forgave him for what happened because he slept in my room. "He says it was a mistake..."

"I don't care about that either. He can do whatever he wants. It's not like he asks me for permission to do whatever he does. He's not my boyfriend, Cesar," I add.

He rears back slightly, and I look at our audience, realizing I said more than necessary. It's the truth, and I'm tired of lying to myself. Being at risk is nothing new. I've lived in danger all my life. No one was there to save me. Everyone moved on, except me. If I was still in foster care when I turned eighteen, I would be sent on my way like they did to him.

I would be homeless, needing to figure out my own shit. My life. With no family and no one I could trust. I'm living here with no job, the least I could do is clean until I get one.

Cesar nods slightly in understanding. "If you want to clean because it's something you feel you need to do, I won't stop you. But you don't have to."

"I'm going to find work, and I'll help out. I got six months until I graduate."

He looks at the guys and then at me. "We'll talk about this later," he says, kissing me on the cheek. "You're beautiful," he whispers. "Remember that."

When Cesar walks away, I wish I could agree with him, but

then, my eyes shift to the guys on the couch, and I know that is further from the truth from how they stare when they think I don't notice. I'm not like the girls that come in and hang around the guys. Pretty, wearing clothes that show their pretty bodies and nice smooth skin.

"Hey." One of the guys calls out, wearing an oversized collared flannel shirt and a shaved head. "What happened?" He points at me with a cigarette before he slides it behind his ear. "You got a pretty face and all, but that looks fucked up." The guy next to him elbows him to keep his mouth shut.

I hear the front door behind me open with a slight groan, but I don't turn around and decide to answer. I'm not ashamed anymore. "My mom was a meth and heroin addict, and so was my stepfather. One day, when I was ten, I used to sneak out to meet this boy. He would wait until I arrived home. When he found out where I went, he forced me to kneel with my shirt off. He hit me with a weathered black belt on my back. They had these little metal rings with holes in them. I think they were afraid I would tell this boy that they abused me. But I liked this boy so much, I took it and didn't stop sneaking out to see him."

The room fills with an awkward silence. The other three guys sitting in the loveseat look at each other with guilty expressions. It's a fucked-up story, but it's mine.

"What happened with the boy?" Shaved head asks.

They all look up, waiting for my answer. "After I was taken away by social services, I was left with scars reminding me that it was all for nothing. Fate had a funny way of showing me how much he moved on when I met him years later. How much he changed and wasn't the boy I thought he was. How he felt about me. How pointless it was to carry a torch for someone when you meant so little that they would hurt you after you suffered to be with them. When you look at me–– judging me by the way I look reminds me how cruel people are. I just... have to get used to it."

The front door finally shuts with a click. I turn around to find Ky and Manny.

Ky looks over at the guys in the living room with a glare. "All of you, get the fuck out."

They all get up, muttering apologies as they file out. Manny stands to the side, avoiding eye contact with me. I'm not surprised. He's just another judgmental prick.

Ky's wearing a tank top showing his muscular arms with his tattoos and sweats pants. He must have come straight from working out at the gym.

"Why are you cleaning?"

"Because that is what you do when something is dirty. This place looked like shit."

"I'll get someone to do it."

"I wanted to," I counter. "It gives me something to do."

His eyes smolder. The black depths hinted at everything he would love for me to do. He grips the mop, but I don't protest and let him take it, placing it against the wall.

"Let's go."

I shake my head. "I don't want to go with you."

"I'm taking you to dinner."

"I'm not hungry."

He steps closer, and I can smell his cologne, making my stomach flip. "Please."

I let him take me out over the weekend, and I couldn't look at him the whole time, and I still can't. The image of him kissing her back played in my mind after he said he loved me.

"I can't."

He licks his bottom lip and looks down at his feet. "I said I was sorry, Rubi. It wasn't..."

I step back, and his eyes meet mine, full of sadness. But I feel broken. "It was exactly what it looked like. She was right. You always go back to her. I was being stupid and didn't believe her. I need space, Ky. I need space so I can find room for you as my friend."

I turn around before I cry in front of him, running into Cesar. A tear escapes my cheek unchecked, and I watch Cesar's face fall, but I smile, trying to hold it all in. "Not everyone thinks the way you do. They just feel guilty," I say softly.

I ran into the bedroom, shutting the door and flicking the lock. I slide down, tucking my knees to my chest, and let the tears fall.

I pull my phone out of the back pocket of my jeans, pull off the headphones, and open the photo app to look at the picture of Ky kissing Jen. Because I'm a glutton for punishment. I shouldn't look when the emotions are raw, like a fresh wound that still bleeds. The picture reminds me to be strong ––To not give in. So I can have the strength to let him go.

CHAPTER TWENTY-ONE
Ky

"YOU GOOD?" Cesar asks, walking back inside.

I nod. "Yeah," I lie. "What did Manny want?" I ask, not ready to talk about the Rubi.

He holds up a stack of cash. "Paying me back for getting to secure his shop."

"He went to school?" I ask.

Cesar plops down on the couch. "Yep. He has this thing that he wants to graduate high school. It's personal."

"Does he say anything about Rubi?"

Cesar shakes his head. "He just got back. Only a few of the guys know about her. I told them to keep an eye on her at school. Why?"

I shrug, shaking my head. "No reason."

Cesar stares at me like he can see right through me. "No reason, huh?" He scratches his forehead like he's piecing a puzzle together. "What are you worried about?"

"Her safety."

He laughs through his nose, shaking his head. "You know... I never pinned you for the jealous type, but I can't say I blame you when it comes to her."

I play dumb. "What are you talking about?"

"You fucked up, and she friend-zoned your ass. Now you're worried about someone else getting her attention."

I scoff. "Whatever, I have nothing to worry about."

He smirks. "Oh yeah, why is that?"

My face tightens, and I look him straight in the eyes. "Because if anyone touches her, I'll cut them up into pieces."

"You think she'll like that?"

I blink.

He sighs. "You hurt her, Ky."

"I didn't mean to."

"But she can't shake what she saw." He points to the hallway and lowers his voice. "She walked out, not caring who saw her scars. Not caring what anyone thinks."

"And?"

Rubi is beautiful; her scars are mine, and I've shown her that. She shouldn't have to worry about what anyone else thinks.

"You don't get it. It means she doesn't care.... she's letting go."

"Letting go of what?" But I do know. I just need to hear it from him because I don't know what to do. I don't know how to fix it. I don't know how to get her back.

"The past... she wants to let go of the past. The hurt. The pain. I hate to say it, but you are part of the past, Ky. You heard what she said when we walked in."

I did and saw the look in her eyes when she turned around. It gutted me, but I won't give up. I would never give up on us, no matter how stuck up my own ass I've been.

"I'm not going to let her go, Cesar. I will never let her go."

"I see that, but it is up to her to decide. And"--fake coughs--"you're going to have to prove that everything she has gone through for you was worth it. Show her."

I slide my hand over my face and look up at the ceiling. "I'm trying, but I don't know how. I'm not good"--I swallow-- "at relationships."

"Me either. I don't have all the answers, and I'm shit at relationships, too," he admits. "But everyone in her life has hurt her in some way."

Including me. I know he wants to say it, but out of respect, he won't, but it hangs in the air.

I get up and head down the hallway. "Where are you going?" he calls out.

"I need to talk to my BFF," I tease.

"*Estas loco*. Good luck."

He says I'm crazy. He isn't wrong. I'm crazy about her.

I knock, knowing I could pick the lock and waltz right in, but I need to give her control.

"Yeah," she says through the door.

I knock louder several times and earn another "Yeah."

I knock again and hear her stomping toward the door, pulling it open with force. "What?"

Her eyes widen when she sees it's me. "You weren't expecting me?" I ask, my chest tightening, seeing her eyes puffy and red from crying and feeling like shit.

My eyes take in the thin camisole and boy shorts. My cock getting the memo. "Do you always answer the door dressed like that?"

"Does it matter?"

I step in, pushing the door wider. "I can see your nipples."

"It's black," she says with a sarcastic smile. "You can't see shit. Now, what do you want?"

I lick my lips, sucking my bottom lip with my teeth. "Everything," I breathe.

She rolls her eyes, but if she only knew how hot she looked, she would dress like that with her lips swollen. Her cheeks flushed. Perky breasts begging for my tongue. Her hips flare out slightly, with a flat stomach, showing an inch of skin I'm dying to lick.

"I'm sure you have no trouble finding"--she makes quotation marks with her fingers-- "everything out there."

"You're right," I smirk. "I found everything I was looking for, but she doesn't believe me."

She throws her hands up frustratingly. "What do you want, Ky?"

"I want to take my best friend out to eat."

Her eyes narrow. "Best friend?"

I clear my throat. "Yeah. You said you needed space for me to be your friend. I'm here to fill it." I pause, hoping this works.

"Friends go out to eat, right?" I lean in slightly and whisper, "We were best friends first, Rubi."

She licks her lips, and I swear my cock weeps inside my boxers. "Friends," she states.

"Friends," I volley back, letting the word roll off my tongue. I never hated a word so much in life before.

She sighs in defeat. "Fine."

I roll my lips, trying to stifle the smile at my small victory. "Is that a yes?"

She rolls her eyes dramatically. "If it gets you to stop being so annoying."

"Bullshit, I know you're hungry." I raise my brows. "Chinese?"

"I hate it when you mess with me, Ky."

I knew she loved Chinese when she first tried it. "Chinese it is. I know just the place."

"Alright, wait here. Let me put something on." She pushes the door, thinking I left. When she turns around, I step inside and close the door, leaning on it. I watch her perky ass in those boy shorts.

When she looks up after finding a pair of jeans, her eyes widen in surprise. "What the hell, Ky?"

I raise my hands in mock surrender. "I'm waiting for you."

"I meant outside."

I smile. "It's too late now. It's not like I haven't seen everything."

She blows a puff of air out her mouth, loving the way she gets all flustered, pushing her leg through and then the other zipping up her jeans. She turns around, and my eyes trace the scars on her back, itching to walk over there, and pepper kisses all over them to remind her she is strong and gorgeous.

She removes her camisole, and it takes everything in me that I possess to not walk over there and lick every inch of her.

When she turns around to face me, she asks harshly, "Did you enjoy the view?"

"I have never seen something more beautiful," I tell her honestly.

"Lying is a sin, you know."

"It's a good thing I'm not lying. I can't be your friend if I lie to you."

After taking her to dinner at the best Chinese restaurant in town, I asked her if she was okay at school. If anyone is giving her trouble. She says she is fine and tells me that Katie and the others are nice. She leaves out that I've slept with all of them, but I see it in her eyes. She knows. It bothers her, and it bothers me that it does, and I feel helpless. Because I couldn't make this go away. I could move her back to my house, but I would have to kill her father to make it happen.

I would do anything for her, but I couldn't stomach her hating me for going through with it. Tyler is in jail. The lawyers think it's a good idea to leave him and not bond him out so that he can serve as much time as he can until the second hearing. Some shit about getting credit for time served.

He is looking at a minimum of nine months to a year for assault and battery. Nine with good behavior and two years' probation. Noah can't speak much with a broken jaw, but he's recovering. Chris's parents went through with the restraining order for Abby, not that she wants anything to do with him to care much about it. She only cares about Noah and hates Tyler for what he did.

Rubi listens quietly, but I see the emotions play in her eyes. She feels bad for everyone.

"I talked to Tyler," I tell her, firing up the car.

"What did he say?"

"That he's sorry. To apologize to Abby and Noah for what he has done. He never meant to hurt Noah." I glance at her. "And... to you."

"Me," she says in a surprised tone.

"He wanted me to tell you that his father is a prick and that he wants nothing to do with the company or the money and that he should leave it all to you."

"That is not a good thing, is it? I never wanted anything except a father."

I shake my head, driving out of the parking lot. "It's not a good thing. It just makes it worse, honestly. I can make it go away."

She looks down at her hands in her lap. "How?"

"I can take care of it."

She pinches her brows. "What do you mean... take care of it?"

"Exactly what it means, Rubi."

"You can't." she shakes her head frantically. "That's... crazy," she cries.

"So is him threatening to get rid of you, but I want to warn you, Rubi. If he attempts anything... I will end him. Hate me or not. I will protect you if that is what it takes."

"You're serious," she grumbles.

"Deadly."

"I don't get it. Why would you risk it all for me?"

"Because...I love you, Rubi. I meant when I said it. I'm going to keep saying it until it sinks in."

"No, you don't. You don't mean it."

"I do, and in time, I'll prove it to you. If I'm with you or not. I love you, Rubi."

She looks out the window, and I know she doesn't believe me. But she will. She is all I think about. She is all I have ever thought about since I met her. I've made mistakes. I've judged her. I've hurt her. I've let her down, but sometimes we make mistakes to learn what matters most. She is what matters most to me. I just need to show her.

CHAPTER TWENTY-TWO
Rubi

"YOU'RE GOOD," The lady in charge of the cafeteria says.

She said I have money in my account to cover anything I want to eat.

"Are you sure?"

She waves her hand, gesturing me to keep walking through the line. "You're covered."

I pick up my tray and head to an empty table and take a seat pulling out my phone to text Ky.

> Rubi: Did you put money in my lunch account at school?"

> Ky: Yeah.

> Rubi: Why?

> Ky: Because you need to eat. Don't argue with me on this. You need to eat Rubi, and I will make sure you do.

> Rubi: You don't have to do that.

> Ky: I did. It's not a big deal.

> Rubi: I'm getting a job and paying you back.

> Ky: You don't have to get a job and pay me back.

> Rubi: I'm getting one. I need to pay my own way.

Ky: I have money, Rubi. More than I need.

Rubi: It's your money, not mine. You don't get it.

He thinks he can just buy me.

Ky: If getting a job makes you feel better, then fine. Let me know where, okay? I need to make sure you're safe.

Rubi: Okay, I'll let you know.

Ky: How's Hope? I left kitty litter and food. Does he miss me?

I smile because I would never have pegged him as a cat person.

Rubi: You like cats?

Ky: I love your kitty, both of them. ;)

Rubi: Very funny.

Ky: I never joke about pussy.

Rubi: I bet you know all about pussy.

Ky: I admit, I do. But there is something about yours that milks me just right.

My cheeks heat. I look around and meet honey-brown eyes watching me across the table.

"Must be a good conversation."

"Huh?"

He points at my tray, my food untouched. "You've been sitting there for about five minutes texting whoever and haven't touched your food. Your cheeks are flushed. Like I said, it must be a good conversation."

I pocket my phone like I was caught looking at something dirty. I look around and notice the guys that hang out with Cesar at another table. I see Katie and Sarah smiling at something one of the guys said. I'm surprised Manny isn't over there.

I turn my head back to my tray and pick up a straw to poke the little juice bag. "Aren't you sitting at the wrong table?"

He places his forearms on the table's edge and opens the wrapper to pull out his spork. "I wasn't aware there was a right table."

I poke the bag of juice. "Won't your friends miss you?"

"Maybe I want to make new friends."

"I think that will be difficult because I'm the only one sitting here. Don't you have a girlfriend or something? There are plenty of girls over there. I'm sure you can find one to keep your lap warm."

"You're not good at this making friends thing, are you?"

"I didn't know I needed a friend."

He twirls the spaghetti with the spork. "I know I judged you the other day. I was quick to assume things about you. I'm sorry."

"You don't have to apologize for being who you are," I say between bites.

He chuckles, shaking his head. "That's cold."

"You don't have to sit here because you feel sorry for me. You can go and sit with your friends."

"Maybe I don't want to sit with them."

I swallow the food in my mouth. "Why is that?"

He shrugs. "Because I want to sit here. The view is better."

Did he just insinuate that he thinks I'm pretty? He has balls knowing Ky and Cesar to say something like that.

"How do you know Ky?"

"Straight to the point," he says, wiping his mouth with a napkin. "Through Cesar."

Makes sense. Cesar knows people in and out of foster care and that he is a few years older. He's been on his own, doing whatever he needs to survive.

"How do you know Cesar?"

"I met him through the guys at school when I moved here from Ohio my sophomore year with my older brother. I had to repeat a grade because I kept skipping school. I was supposed to graduate last year. How do you know Cesar?"

I bite my lip, keeping true to what I tell everyone.

"Foster care."

"It takes guts to admit what you said the other day. The boy. It was Ky, wasn't it?"

I shift in my seat, staring at my plate, not knowing what to say. I forgot he was there when the guy with the shaved head asked about my scars.

"You heard enough."

"I did." I look up. "I'm ashamed I didn't see it before."

I draw my brows in. "See what?"

"What the perfect girl would look like."

I push up my sleeves on my arms to give me something to do. I've never been told I was perfect before. "I think freak is more accurate," I mutter.

"You like daisies?"

"Huh?" I heard him but forgot about my tattoos and that he's an artist.

His eyes trail up to my elbow. I pull my arm away, trying to hide them from his gaze.

"You like daisies," he repeats. "They're pretty. How were you able to get them done? You must have just turned eighteen. Whoever the artist was did a good job. I don't agree with the letters, though."

"Cesar knew this tattoo artist when I told him what I wanted. It was before he met Ky. His name was Dereck."

Manny grins, and I agree with Katie; he is nice to look at. He has straight white teeth, a nice smile, a chiseled jaw, and a nicely shaped nose. His arms are inked with skulls and angels on tight skin over lean muscle. He is tall with wide shoulders and fills out his black shirt. Ky is bigger and more muscular with a darker appeal. Dangerous. Manny seems...safe.

"Dereck, did your sleeve?"

I nod slowly. "Yeah. Cesar hooked me up."

"It's a small world."

"Why is that?" I ask curiously.

"Because Dereck's my older brother. We own a shop together."

I smile in surprise. "Really?"

"Yeah," he says with a laugh.

"He's a nice guy. I wish I could say the same about you."

He places his hand over his chest. "I'm not that bad once you get to know me."

A thought pops into my head, and I clear my throat. "After I get a job, I want to ask if he could cover something up for me."

Manny tilts his head to the side. "What do you want to cover up?"

I lick my lips nervously. "The letters. I want to cover them up with another daisy."

He raises his brows. "I was just kidding about the name."

"It's not about that."

His eyes soften. "Then what is it about?"

"I want to let go of the past."

He leans closer with his elbows on the table, lowering his voice. "Are you sure that's what you really want?"

I smile wryly. "Yeah, I do."

After the bell rings at the end of the day, I make my way out toward the student parking lot, where Cesar is waiting, talking with a couple of guys.

"Rubi!" I turn and see Katie rushing over with a beaming smile.

She reminds me of Abby. All smiles, wishing the guy she's fallen for would feel the same. Sometimes, I've been tempted to call her to see how she's doing, but I know that would draw unwanted attention if she said anything at school.

"Hey."

"I wanted to tell you the good news. I got you a job. It's nothing big, but it's a start and after school. I hope you like pizza. It's a cashier position, so you don't have to cook or anything like that. All you have to do is show up and fill out the paperwork, and the job is yours. Twelve bucks an hour Monday thru Friday from four pm to close," she rushes out.

I'm shocked she looked out for me. "Is that okay?" She asks with a grimace.

"Oh...yes. Of course! I was just shocked you found something so fast, is all."

She lets out a sigh. "Thank God. I thought you were disappointed in me."

"Never. I'm just not used to someone doing something for me when they've only known me for a short time. Thank you, Katie."

"It's no biggie. I'm glad I could help." I watch her look over at Cesar. One of the girls is standing close to him with her hand on his chest, hanging on to every word he says. His smile tells me he's interested as far as her legs can open. I know Cesar. I know when he is genuine toward someone.

"You have nothing to worry about," I tell her. "He doesn't like her––not like that."

She gives me a watery smile. "That's Tammy. She is always gloating when she sleeps with him. How good he is in bed."

"He's not that good," I mutter, and my face falls, wanting to take back the words.

Shit.

Her head whips around. "You..."

"Shit," I grumble. "Katie...I."

She waves her hand. "Who hasn't. I mean, it's the same with Ky, right?"

She isn't wrong, and she did admit the same, but I don't want to hurt her feelings. "Yeah, I guess you could say that. But it wasn't like that with me and Cesar. Something bad happened to me one night, and he was there."

"What happened?"

"Yeah, what happened?" I hear a familiar voice and Katie's squeal.

"Nothing, just girl talk," she says to Manny, giving him a friendly hug.

But I notice he's looking at me from the corner of my eye, not missing that Cesar is looking straight at us. His eyes flick to Katie

with, her hands wrapped around Manny's neck with a big smile plastered on her face.

"I love girl talk," Manny says. My gaze reaches his, noticing a playful glint in his eyes.

"I'm sure you hear plenty of girls talk."

"Nothing that interests me until you."

I feel my body burning up. My thoughts go to Ky, wondering what girl he's with or if he took Jen to school this morning, and I quickly berate myself for being stupid. We're just friends. He can do whatever he wants.

Katie pulls away from Manny, fanning herself. "Is it still hot in November, or just me."

"We were just talking about Tammy and how she gloats about screwing Cesar," I tell him, changing the subject.

Manny looks over at Tammy with Cesar and snorts. "Who? Tammy?" He sucks his teeth. "She's a mutt bucket."

"A what?" I ask. "What the hell is a mutt bucket?" I look over to see if I missed something but only notice that Cesar stepped away from her.

"It's what guys call an easy lay. She screws anyone with influence or what people deem popular. That's why she gloats. She knows Cesar is connected. He knows that and every guy that has slept with her. She'll do anything. Don't get me wrong, I have nothing against girls who like to have safe sex and all, but they don't usually gloat about who they sleep with like it's a game they won."

I got that vibe from looking at Cesar's reaction to her, but for Manny to point it out makes it true.

"Then why sleep with her?" Katie asks.

I know she's hurt about Cesar, but he's complicated. He cares. He knows what he does for money, and the life he leads leaves no room for a nice girl in his life.

Manny squints at her, probably making the same assumption I did. "Because she's not important, and guys have needs. It doesn't mean anything."

"Girls have needs, too, you know," she replies.

Manny's gaze lands on me. "Do they?"

My thoughts fly to the night I saw Ky kissing Jen, and her words echo in the back of my mind, twisting my gut. *He always comes back to me.*

"They do. We just don't talk about it the way guys do." His eyes darken like a bar of chocolate.

"How do girls satisfy themselves without anyone finding out?"

"We wait for the right moment-- that special moment. The one that she is sure of. She doesn't need to share the one because it's better to keep it a secret."

He closes the distance. "How do girls know when it's the right moment?"

Katie looks between us, the tension building in the air around us. "A girl just knows... It needs to feel right. Some girls, but not all. Not girls like Tammy."

"How about you?" He asks. "What would it take to feel right?"

"Okay, you two..." Katie cuts in, making me take a step back. "I'm about to burst into flames listening to you guys go at it."

My cheeks heat, wanting the ground to swallow me whole. What the hell am I doing?

Manny smiles, holding my gaze. "I'll find out." He walks by me and whispers, "Oh, and if you're worried about your scars, don't because I think they're beautiful. We all have scars, Rubi. They tell a story of who we are and how far we are willing to go." And he walks away.

"Jesus," Katie mumbles under her breath.

I watch him walk away toward his black Mustang. "What?"

"The way he looks at you is...intense."

I feign indifference. "He's just flirting. All guys flirt."

"Not like that, they don't. There is no doubt he wants to bend you over and fuck your brains out, but he genuinely likes you, Rubi."

"No, he doesn't. He judged me the moment he saw me for the first time."

"That's because a rich girl back in Ohio played him. He was good to fuck but not good enough to meet the parents."

"That sucks."

"Yeah, it does. It's a shame because he is fine and doesn't have a girlfriend."

I feel bad for him now hearing about his story, so I ask, "Why is that?"

"I don't know, but I think I overheard that he still loves her. I don't think he ever got over it."

I understand him because I have the same problem. I tried to go out with Chris and move on, but I couldn't because Ky was there sucking me back in, refusing to let him go.

CHAPTER TWENTY-THREE
Rubi

IT'S MY SECOND WEEK, and I smell like cheese and bread. I swear the smell is embedded in my hair no matter how often I wash it. "That will be thirty-two fifty-three, please." The lady swipes her card and hands her the receipt. "It will be out in just a minute."

The phone rings. "Thank you for calling Pizza Hut. This is Rubi. Will it be carryout or delivery?"

"We're going to get you, bitch," a man says in a hard voice and hangs up. I checked the caller ID, and it's blocked.

A sinking feeling settles low in my stomach at all the threats I've received since I started. I wonder how they found me or if it's a prank to scare me.

"Order number 572!" John calls out.

I pull out the two steaming boxes of pizza, almost gagging at the smell of anchovies.

"Number 572!" I call out. Prompting the lady with the red hair to step forward with her two kids. "Here you go."

When Katie gave me the address to the job, she put in a good word for me to start. When I saw it was at a Pizza Hut, I froze for five minutes, not caring about the sun burning a hole in my back from walking the mile and a half to get there. I didn't want to ask Cesar for a ride, and I'm glad I didn't. I knew he would pick up on my reaction when I saw the place. I hadn't slept well since I started and kept it from Ky. When he asked why I wasn't home, I told him I had to study with Katie at her house. I was grateful he didn't push. I keep having nightmares that Mike is still out to get me with a box of Pizza Hut.

I felt stupid when I woke up, remembering why I was so scared, but it's good to face things that have plagued me in the past. Something I hated and was ashamed of as a little girl. I still can't bring myself to eat it, but it's part of letting go and not dwelling on things like not having the right parents or the privilege other kids had growing up. I want to improve and strive for a future, whatever that entails. I want to heal.

When it's almost closing time, the manager, Tom, places a white envelope with my name on the counter. "It's payday." I smile. "You're doing an excellent job," Tom says.

"Thank you." He nods and then hands me two-hundred-dollar bills. I look up. "What..."

"Tips. I'm not supposed to do that in cash, but it's just this one time," he says, giving me a wink.

A couple of friends are looking out for me more than they should. I pocket the money and clock out next door, taking off the black hat and untucking my shirt.

The sound of the bell rings when I open the door, the smell of antiseptic, a welcome change to the smell of Pizza from next door.

The first day I started, I was surprised that Manny and Dereck's tattoo shop was next door. A little detail Katie left out, but I wasn't upset. I was relieved I knew someone close by, just in case. I haven't told Ky or Cesar about the threatening phone calls. I haven't told anyone. I know it's stupid, but I like the feeling of independence. Everyone stays out of my way, and I finally have space.

Ky still sends food and litter for Hope, but he's giving me space. He has dinner and breakfast delivered during the week and shows up on the weekends.

"Hey," Dereck says with a smile. "How was work?"

"Good, I guess. I got paid."

"That's what counts, right?"

I nod, looking at the piece he's working on for a customer. I turn toward Manny's station but don't see him.

"He's in the private room on a call. He'll be out in just a minute."

"Oh, that's okay. I came to talk to you."

He places the drawing pencils down. "Oh." I smile. "What do you want to talk about?" He asks.

Dereck doesn't look like Manny; he's more rugged, with piercings on his nose and lips. He has way more tattoos on his neck and looks much older, reminding me of the Sons of Anarchy with the wallet chain and boots. It makes it hard to believe they're related at all.

I hold out my arm with the daisies he did when I just turned seventeen. "I wanted to cover up the letters. It's not big, but since you did the work, I thought it was best if you did the cover-up. It could be another daisy. A darker one."

"Are you sure?" He asks, looking at me with a worried expression.

"I'm sure."

"This isn't causing me any trouble, is it?"

I shake my head. "It won't..."

"I'm done. You need to stop calling me...no––" I look toward the back room. Manny has his back turned. "I don't want you to come down for Thanksgiving. We're not together anymore. What part of that don't you understand," he says in frustration. "It's not because of someone else. Look, I can't do this with you right now, Brittney. I gotta go." Manny turns, pocketing his phone, and our eyes meet for a second. I see a flash of guilt, but I must have imagined it. Katie was right. He's still hung up on his girlfriend.

Dereck gives me a tight smile, but I return to why I'm here. "Like I said, it won't cause any trouble, but if you can't, I understand." I chew on my lip nervously, realizing I shouldn't have asked. I shouldn't have come here. There are dozens of tattoo artists. I'll find someone else.

"I-I'm sorry, Dereck," I stammer nervously. "I shouldn't have come and asked."

"Rubi, it's okay," Dereck says, but I walk backward toward the exit, embarrassment eating me.

197

"I should have never come here. I'm sorry."

"Rubi, wait," Manny rushes toward me before I walk out, his expression softening. "What did you need?"

"Nothing, I came at a bad time."

"It's not a bad time. Tell me."

"She wanted to cover up the name on her forearm," Dereck answers. "Maybe you should do it, brother. It will help get your mind off other things."

"Can I see?"

I hold my forearm out for him to take a closer look. "If you feel uncomfortable..."

He slides his hand into mine, lacing his fingers. "Come."

"Now?"

"Yeah, I have nothing better to do right now. Besides, I'm finished with the piece I was working on."

He tugs me along, cleans the chair with antiseptic, and prepares the area. I sit, and he takes my arm in his hand and studies the two black letters from a man that people fear, but Manny isn't afraid of covering it up for some reason. He doesn't look worried or scared of Ky.

"Do you know what daisies symbolize?" I shake my head. "True love––the innocence of love." I look away, my eyes filling with tears, but he continues, "There are two parts"––he traces his finger over one–– "center floret and then the outer floret. When they blend together, they form complete harmony. That is why they symbolize true love. It is why the game he loves me/he loves me not is played with the outer florets." My chest squeezes when the image of dark eyes watching me pull a petal plays in my mind on a loop. "It's innocent because it's pure."

I blink back to keep from making a fool out of myself and cry in front of him. "I didn't know that."

"I have an idea. If you want..."

"Okay."

"The daisies are black and white, and since the letters are black but not that big, I could place a red tulip over it in bright red."

"What does a red tulip mean," I blurt, already loving the idea.

"Red tulips mean love, passion, and lust. They also mean true feelings...the truth of love. They also grow amongst the daisies in the spring."

"How do you know all this?"

"That's easy. I was curious as to why you got them." He pulls his drawing pad out and shows me a red tulip.

"I love it. It's perfect."

Manny's eyes darken, and there is something familiar about him that I can't place.

"Then, let's get started."

CHAPTER TWENTY-FOUR
Ky

"I KNOW WHERE SHE WORKS," Cesar says, leaning against his car.

I told him to meet me by the abandoned warehouses to avoid discussing anything about Rubi at the house.

"Where?"

"You're not going to like it."

I look up at the dark sky. "This is what I get for giving her space like she wanted."

"She seems okay with it, I guess. Considering——"

"Considering what?"

"She's working at Pizza Hut."

I almost choke on my spit. "What the fuck, Cesar?"

"I know...but maybe... it isn't bad."

"Like fuck it is! She hates that place. I hate that fucking place for her."

Cesar rubs his chin. "He watches her and makes sure she's safe."

"I'm sure he does," I spit, my voice dripping with jealousy.

"Relax, he was with that Brittney chick last weekend, or was it the one before?"

"That was to humiliate her and make her suffer for thinking he was a low life," I grit.

"He's your brother, Ky."

"Half-brother. Just because we came out of the same ball sack doesn't mean he won't go after Rubi. I warned him already."

Cesar gives me a look like I'm overreacting. "I saw how he looked at her when we showed up, and she was cleaning."

"What look?" Cesar asks, playing dumb.

"The one that will get a bullet to his head. It's bad enough that I learned about his existence when my father told me I had a brother and wasn't his only son. My father knocked up his mother before I came along and married my mother, thinking he could keep it hidden."

"Hey, players fuck up," he teases. I give him a murderous glare. "Alright, alright. It was a joke."

"It's gonna be a joke when I paint the tattoo shop with his fucking brain for touching her and then have to explain to my father why he has to bury his bastard son."

"Manny won't let anything happen to her. He's trained like you are."

"I bet he has something to do with getting her a job there."

"Possibly, *Hermano*. But he doesn't know her story."

"Any word on her stepfather?"

"He's around. Got out of jail last month. He's sniffing to score. Once an addict and all that."

"Good, I'll let Manny come along this time. Maybe he'll understand."

Cesar scoffs. "What? Spit it out, asshole."

"Marry her."

"It's not that simple."

"It is. Talk to whoever you need to...grandfather or whoever, and tell them you want to marry Rubi. She'll be protected. If they kill her father, fuck it. It won't be on your hands."

I've thought about it. I've thought about it a lot, but that would mean I would have to get involved in the family business. I don't know if Rubi is ready for that type of life.

"Funny."

"What's so funny?"

"You...giving me advice about Rubi in a dark alley by an abandoned warehouse."

"I love her. I want her to be happy. Is that so hard to under-stand? I would marry her, but I can't protect her like you can."

My nostrils flare, but I know he is just messing with me so I can make the calls and get it going.

"How about Katie?"

His jaw tics. "What about her?"

"You still mad I slept with her, aren't you?"

"I'm not."

"Yes, you are. In the same way, I'm mad you were Rubi's first."

"I told you why..."

I raise a hand to stop him. I know why. We've talked about this a hundred times.

"I get it. So why are you such a dick to Katie? She's been cool and has been nice to Rubi."

"I told you. She's clingy."

"Alright, I'll introduce her to Chris then. Get his mind off shit with his sister and the whole Tyler mess."

"The fuck you will."

I smirk. "She is going to fuck somebody, Cesar." I open the driver's side door of my BMW. "She's not a nun. Maybe my brother would like a crack at it."

"If he touches her, I'll put a bullet in his head myself," he seethes.

I raise a brow.

He pauses and runs his fingers in his hair in frustration. "I know how you feel."

"No, you don't. But you'll see." I nudge my chin toward his car. "Go get your girl before someone else does."

"She's not my girl. I'm waiting for you to fuck up so I can love Rubi the way she deserves."

"You have a death wish, don't you."

"She deserves the world, Ky. I'm going to make sure she gets it. If you want to kill me for wanting that for her, fine. But she'll hate you."

"You're such a prick."

He smiles. "That's why you trust me with her."

He isn't wrong. He'll protect Rubi like I would with his life.

I dial my father as soon as I'm in the car. His secretary answers answering in fluent Italian.

"Put him on," I demand. She knows not to question me when I call.

I hear movement and hushed voices, and then, "Ky?"

"I need the plane."

"For?"

"Italy."

"Son––"

"I know what you'll say, but I need to talk with my grandfather."

"You're ready to take over?"

"As long as Rubi becomes my wife."

"You're young Ky. Give it time…"

"I'm done giving it time. She is living in a house with drug dealers. She shouldn't be around that stuff or a shit school."

"You know we're no different. It's not like we're curing cancer, son."

"I know that, but we don't live inside where we shit, do we?"

"You're brother Manny…"

"Half-brother," I correct. "And he has a problem keeping his eyes to himself."

My father chuckles. "He does have a soft spot."

"I don't care, but I can't protect her like this. She's working at Pizza Hut."

"Alright, but you realize her life will change, Ky. Bodyguards, marriage, and your brother…"

"Will what?"

I get annoyed every time he mentions him like I owe him something. He's related to me through my father, but it doesn't mean I have to go camping with him and sing songs by the fire.

"He will take his place by your side. He won't be at the head, but he will have a place, Ky."

"I don't care. I just need to end this before they make a move, and I'm too late. I won't forgive myself if something happens to her."

"Call Manny and make sure he watches over her. Cesar can't keep an eye on her and run things simultaneously. The plane will be ready in two hours."

I hang up and pull into the driveway, knowing everything will change once I speak to my grandfather. I don't even know what he looks like in person. I've only seen him in the pictures my father has shown me. My grandfather, Augustine Mancini, is the head of the Italian mafia. One of the most feared families in the world, and I will walk in and demand to be his successor if he gives me the blessing to marry the girl I have loved since I was ten years old. I just hope he will.

———

I walk inside my grandfather's home in Italy after being driven for two hours by three black Mercedes SUVs following the outskirts of the quiet Italian village. I couldn't help but feel a sense of both anticipation and trepidation. The cobbled streets wound toward the countryside, leading me to a secluded villa among Tuscany's rolling hills.

The villa, an ancient stone structure with a warm, earthy facade, exuded an air of timeless grandeur. Ivy and bougainvillea crept up the walls, adding a touch of vibrant color to the rustic exterior. The main entrance was flanked by two enormous oak doors, their ironwork crafted with symbols and patterns that spoke of the rich history of the Mancini family.

As I stepped inside ahead of the bodyguards dressed in black suits in a spacious foyer, the cool crème Italian marble floors underfoot starkly contrasted the warm, welcoming atmosphere. Antique furniture, richly upholstered in deep burgundy and dark wood, filled the room. Paintings of Italian landscapes, some dating back centuries, adorned the walls, and soft golden light from wrought-iron chandeliers cast a glow over the surroundings.

The interior was a mix of old-world charm and modern

convenience. A grand staircase with an ornate handrail led to the upper levels, where rooms branched off in every direction. It was clear that every detail had been carefully chosen, from the hand-woven rugs to the intricate crown moldings that adorned the ceilings.

I was shown to a study by an older woman, an expansive room with towering bookshelves, mahogany paneling, and a fireplace that crackled with warmth. My grandfather sat like a patriarch behind a massive desk. His presence was commanding, a testament to the years of influence and power he had held with dark hair pitch black like mine. Except his hair around the temples had a touch of grey.

The room was adorned with more artifacts that spoke of his grandfather's history, a globe that hinted at international connections, leather-bound volumes that held the family's secrets, and a humidor filled with cigars, their rich aroma lingering in the air. The desk was cluttered with papers and documents, a stark reminder of the responsibilities and dealings that came with his position.

My grandfather finally locked eyes with mine; I couldn't ignore the emotions swirling within his dark orbs. Though a place of undeniable luxury, the villa also carried the weight of a complex and dangerous family legacy. A legacy I would be a part of.

"Welcome, my son. It's about time."

"Yes, I guess it is."

He nods, reaching for a cigar. "Have a seat."

I step forward and sit, hating the eight-thousand-dollar suit I'm forced to wear. "Thank you for seeing me on such short notice."

His eyes lift, mirroring the darkness I've held inside me since I was a kid, trying to figure out its origin. This need for hate. It's a need for vehemence and control. It hits me all with a blunt force. The reason my mother left. The reason she begged my father to keep me away. I understand all of it because I can feel it in his gaze. The energy that calls to me tells me I made it home.

"We have things to discuss, Ky."

"We do."

He nods, cutting the cigar with a cutter just like I've seen my father do countless times. "You want to take your place, but you want something."

I straighten. "Yes, sir. She's important to me."

"So I've heard."

"There is one thing I need you to secure first. No questions asked."

"Name it."

"You're in a hurry."

"I am."

"Very well."

"I have a list of things I require, and if you agree, you'll have my blessing." He holds my gaze and continues, "You realize you are a very powerful man, Ky, a Mancini through and through. I see the same hunger inside you I had when I was your age. The need to control. To kill if necessary. To destroy. To take. All in the heat of madness." He lights up the cigar, turning it in the flame so it burns evenly. "She needs to understand what it is to be a Mancini-- Branding her as one."

"How so?"

There is no going back.

This is it.

This is where I make Rubiana mine forever.

"Her loyalty--"

"Has been proven."

"How."

I smile. "I'll tell you. When I was ten years old--"

CHAPTER TWENTY-FIVE
Rubi

"WHERE ARE WE GOING?" I ask Manny sitting in the passenger side of his car after we left his tattoo shop admiring the beautiful red tulip.

"I thought you might be hungry."

I look down at my work clothes. "I'm still dressed in my uniform and still smell like cheese and bread."

"It hasn't bothered me for that last couple of hours if that's what you're worried about. If I drop you off now, you won't eat. Not with all the guys smoking out front and drinking."

He had a point. There's no way I can cook myself something this late. It's almost two in the morning.

"Alright, what did you have in mind?"

"I know a place," he says with a smile pressing the gas reminding me of Ky.

There are things Manny does that reminds me of Ky. It's odd but I can't put my finger on it. The way he stares at me so intense. The same way Ky does. It's like they can both see inside your soul.

He ends up driving to a burger joint. The sound of his car drawing attention to the people seated outside.

The place has a feel of an old diner that sells burgers and shakes. The bright neon sign, adorned with bright red and yellow lights that reads, "Joe's Diner & Burger Shack," reflecting on the sidewalk. We are greeted by the soft jingle of an old-fashioned bell.

Inside, a checkerboard linoleum floor sprawled out beneath rows of well-worn vinyl booths and chrome-edged stools lined up along a gleaming counter. The booths were upholstered in classic red and white, showcasing small tears and patches of history but looks comfortable. The stainless-steel countertop, though showing signs of age, gleamed with character.

On the walls, vintage Coca-Cola ads, black-and-white photographs of local celebrities, and framed newspaper clippings chronicled the diner's rich history. A jukebox, standing proudly in one corner, filled the air with a soothing medley of Elvis Presley, Johnny Cash, and Buddy Holly tunes.

The aroma of sizzling beef patties and fried onions hung in the air, mingling with the familiar scent of freshly brewed coffee and homemade pies. A short-order cook, dressed in a white apron and paper hat, worked diligently behind the counter, flipping burgers on a sizzling griddle and expertly assembling orders with a flourish.

Patrons occupied the booths and counter stools, engaged in hearty conversations or quietly savoring their meals. The sound of laughter, clinking glasses, and the occasional clatter of dishes draws my attention and my stomach sinks when I notice Jen and Nicole from West Lake Prep surrounded by cheerleaders. I look around relieved that I don't see Ky.

Friendly servers, wearing classic diner uniforms, deftly balanced trays full of steaming plates and mugs give us a nod. One of the servers looks up after setting a tray down. "It just the two of you?"

"Yeah," Manny says with a nod.

"You can take a seat anywhere you like. The menu is on the chalk board up top."

We take a seat at a booth on the other side noticing some of the guys from our high school.

"This place is divided," Manny says.

"It looks that way," I answer not missing the way Jen and her friends are laughing looking this way. They must be laughing it up because of what happened at the party. I try not to think about that night. *He's a friend, Rubi. It doesn't matter.*

"You know them?" Manny asks.

I meet his gaze. "Cheer team from West Lake Prep. The bitch

to the left." Manny snorts. "The pretty stuck up one is Jen. Ky's favorite." His looks over and I watch Nicole sitting on the right trying to give her best attempt at a sexy smile.

When his eyes meet mine, he surprises me when he says, "I don't think they're all that. They look like stuck up bitches riding on daddies' money."

"I don't think that matters when they're on their knees."

He raises his eyebrows in surprise and then smiles. "Trust me, they have nothing on you, and I haven't seen you on your knees."

"You don't have to be nice to me because I'm sitting in front of you."

"Do you bust every guy's balls when they pay you a compliment?"

The waiter shows up just in time and we place our order. Plain burger with cheese and an ice cream chocolate shake. I look at the servers passing by excited to try the burger and shake. I've never had one like that before.

"Hungry?" He asks watching me.

My cheeks pink. "I'm sorry. I've never been here before."

He leans back studying me for a few seconds. "It's like every burger and shake place except, the shakes here are pretty good."

I grab the ketchup and mustard and place them closer on the table giving me something to do. I lick my lips nervously. "I've never been," I say truthfully.

My eyes lift, his gaze holds mine. "Here?" He asks with a curiosity.

I rub my lips together. "I've never been to a burger and shake place before."

Realization dawns. "Oh." He straightens in his seat probably thinking I'm weird.

Probably thinking what kind of person has never been to a burger and shake place before. I give him a grin to ward off the awkward silence. He looks over at the chalk board and waves the waiter over.

"Can we have the loaded cheese fries?"

"Sure." The waiter writes it on his order pad and walks away. I reach in my pocket. "What are you doing?" He asks when I pull out money. "Put that away," he demands with a chuckle. "You're giving me a complex over here. All the guys from school are staring at me sitting with you and your pulling out money to pay for the meal."

I look up. "Huh?" I heard him but he must be joking.

He shakes his head and then looks at my hand. "Please?"

I sigh, putting the money away. "Are you going to let me pay for anything?"

He didn't let me pay for the tattoo or for gas. Now he doesn't want me to pay for my meal.

"I have money, Rubi. Plenty."

"Tattoo artist must make good money, huh?"

He snorts and looks away. One of the guys from school walks up to out table. "What's up, Manny?" He turns to me. "Rubi, right?"

"Yeah," I reply.

"I'm Hector. I've heard a lot about you."

"Really?" I ask in surprise.

He nods with a smile and then looks at Manny. "It takes a fine ass girl to get you to come out, eh?"

Manny gaze meets mine when he replies, "Is that your excuse to come over her to get a better look?"

Hector shrugs. "I was hoping you were fucking up and she was bored."

Manny laughs but it doesn't reach his eyes. "You have a death wish."

"I meant no disrespect."

Manny nudges his head toward Jen and her friends. "She thinks those girls giggling over there from West Lake Prep are pretty."

I want to die. I feel like sliding under the table and hiding. Hector looks over and swats his hand sucking his teeth. "Those chicks are wack. Your boy said the one to the right is a dead fuck and the other one does whatever they tell her to do and she's horrible at it. Mutt buckets." Hector' eyes swing to me. "Sorry for

212

the crude remark against females but I'm calling it like it is. They're nothing special." I grin. "If Manny fucks up let me know."

"Get out of here before I slit your throat." Hector laughs but the way Manny says it, causes a chill to snake up my spine.

"Alright, catch you later at school. Bye, Rubi." And he walks away.

"Told you," he says with a mischievous look in his eyes.

I groan at how stuffed I am once we are in the car on our way to Cesar's house. "I'm so full, I think I'm going to explode. Burger, fries and chocolate is going to come pouring out of me all over your nice car."

Manny chuckles. " You didn't eat it all."

"Are you kidding, there was so much food. I did like the shakes though. It was delicious. Thank you."

He smiles. "You're welcome."

He stops are a four-way street and my phone slips through the crack between the center console and the leather seat. "Shit."

We reach in at the same time to get it bumping our heads. "Oh, shit! I'm sorry, Rubi." He grabs my head with both hands' inspection the damage. I can see a little red lump forming on his forehead this close. His eyes roam my face. "Are you okay?" He asks softly, his breath fanning my lips.

"Yes," I whisper.

His head leans close. His eyes fall to my lips and my heart begins to beat wildly in my chest. He smells of chocolate and amber. "Your beautiful, Rubi," he says his lips almost touching mine. I close my eyes bracing for his lips to touch mine, then, the sound of a horn beeping breaks us apart.

Shit.

He places the car in gear and drives. Silence blankets the car as embarrassment washes over me. Thoughts of Ky and what almost happened. I almost kissed Manny and I'm not sure I wanted to or not, but it felt right. He makes me feel safe.

When he pulls up to the house, I turn to face him before I get out. "Thank you for the tattoo and the food. I really had a nice time."

"The daisies look better now. I hope it earns me another date."

I grin. "Are you saying you took me out on a date tonight?"

He wraps a tattooed hand over the top of the steering wheel. "I guess I am."

I open the door and step out and bend down so our eyes meet. "Don't worry. You didn't fuck it up." I shut the door and walk in the house with a huge smile on my face.

When I walk inside, Cesar is sitting on the couch with Katie.

"Who has you smiling like that?" Cesar asks in a playful tone. "More importantly, where have you been?"

"I got a ride from Manny." Katie grins trying to hide it from Cesar.

He checks his phone. "At four thirty in the morning?"

I roll my eyes dramatically. "He gave me a tattoo?"

"Is that all he gave you?"

I arch a brow. "Is there a problem?"

Cesar shakes his head but something flickers in his eyes. I can't place it but it's looks like he's worried. "Be careful, *Nena*."

"Why? Is there something I did wrong?"

Katie looks between me and Cesar. "Manny is good guy," she chimes in.

"That's not it and it's not her I'm worried about."

Ky. He's worries about Ky. But there is no me and Ky anymore.

"Ky and me...we're just friends. He knows that. There is nothing to worry about. I'm not." He leans back on the couch, his eyes watching me like he doesn't believe a word I've said. I sigh not wanting to talk about it. "I'm going to go shower and head to bed."

"Can I see the tattoo," Katie asks. She lets out a gasp when I show her my forearm. "It's beautiful! I love the red tulip."

Cesar sits up and stares at it. Disbelief crossing his features.

He looks up, his eyes meeting mine. "You covered it," he says, but I see the accusation in his eyes.

He knows how bad I wanted to get the daisies with the two letters. He didn't know what it meant at the time because I lied telling him it symbolized a quote I read. He didn't know Ky at the time and never put two and two together. Because in his mind, there was no way I would know a guy like him.

"I did."

He places his hand over his mouth knowing that Ky wouldn't like what I did but there are a lot of things that Ky has done that I don't like.

"Rubi, I know you're hurting but are you sure that was the right thing to do?"

"I think it looks nice," Katies chimes in.

"I agree but..." he trails off.

"It's done. I can't go to the sink and wash it off. I made a decision and I don't regret it."

"Alright, but he's going to lose his shit when he sees it."

I look around mockingly. "He's not here." Katies giggles.

"Get some sleep," Cesar says shaking his head with a grin.

"Yes, dad," I mock, walking toward my room.

CHAPTER TWENTY-SIX
Rubi

KNOCK. *Knock. Knock. Knock.*

I groan, peeling my eyes open. I checked my phone, and it was three in the afternoon. I woke up, took another shower, fed Hope, and fell asleep. I check my text messages, and there is one from Manny.

Manny: Checking up on you. I hope you slept well. Let me know how the tattoo is going. Make sure to clean it and apply the ointment. See you soon.

Knock. Knock.

I swing my legs over. It's probably Manny. I open the door with a big smile. "Hey." But my smile falls.

I step back when he walks inside, shutting the door. "Were you expecting someone else?"

"I don't know what you're talking about, Ky," I lie.

"You don't look happy to see me."

I move my arm back, still wrapped in clear plastic. His gaze catches it, and his mouth turns into a slight frown. His eyes go pitch black, and I brace myself for his reaction. I didn't do it to hurt him. I did it to let go. To move on.

He steps forward and pulls my hand cautiously. "Let me see it." He swallows, and I can hear his heart breaking like glass cracking. His eyes trace the red tulip covering his name in a bed of daisies. His fingers gently caress the skin outside the plastic.

The room goes quiet. The silence is heavy while he stares at it, like memorizing every detail or trying to see if it's a trick, and his name suddenly appears on my skin.

My chest squeezes.

When he looks up, our eyes meet, and my lungs seize. Tears fall down his cheeks from the dark depths of his eyes. My bottom lip trembles when he tries to blink them back. He tries to wipe them away, but they keep falling like a broken dam.

My phone goes off from an incoming message. He walks to the wooden nightstand, and my pulse beats pounding in my ears when he leans over. I swallow thickly.

"Get dressed," he demands, unplugging my phone and sliding it into his back pocket.

"Why? And give me back my phone."

He smiles. His cheeks are still wet, but his eyes are like dark storms ready to destroy everything in his path, and I'm the boat trying not to sink.

"You know why. I'm not going to ask again."

I do as he says, not wanting to cause Manny trouble. I try to tell myself nothing happened, but guilt claws at my insides at what I almost did. The fact that I erased him off my skin hurt him. It cut him deep like the wounds on my back. I just hope I can survive what comes next. I have nowhere to go. I don't have money even if I wanted to leave. And my father wants me dead.

"Where are we going?" I ask him once we are in his car.

The smell of leather and his spicy cologne was familiar, and all Ky. I look through the side mirror and notice a black SUV following close behind.

"It's a surprise."

"Someone is following us."

"I know."

"Is...is that bad?"

"No." He turns to look at me briefly. "You'll get used to it."

Used to what? Is he out of his mind? But I know the answer. He can be.

He glances at the rearview mirror and then straight ahead until we end up parked in front of Pizza Hut, where I work.

I hear car doors slam from behind us, and two men in black

suits with tattoos of stars on their necks walk up to the car, one on each side, and open the doors.

"What is going on, Ky?"

He doesn't answer and slides out of the car. Fuck. I step out, and the man in the suit nods, but I don't miss his hard gaze and olive skin. He walks behind me when I follow Ky, but he walks toward the tattoo shop instead of entering where I work. Manny's Tattoo Shop.

Damn it.

"Ky?" I call out, but the man in the suit opens the door and waits for Ky and me to enter. "Ky?" I call out again, but he ignores me.

He's going to kick his ass, and it's all my fault. I'm so stupid. I rush behind Ky, but it's too late. Manny is seated working on a guy's arm, but his gaze doesn't falter when he notices Ky and the men in suits. Instead, he grins and continues to work on the man's arm. The sound of the tattoo gun buzzing.

"Took you long enough," Manny says, surprising me. "How are you, princess? Sleep well."

Dereck walks out from the back, his eyes round like saucers, when he spots Ky and the men.

"Get everyone out," Ky tells Dereck in a calm tone.

Dereck nods without question, moving around the shop and telling everyone there has been an emergency and that they will get a discount.

"Ky, don't." But he doesn't answer. Hell, he doesn't look at me.

"You know, it's rude to come and disrupt a place of business," Manny says, unfazed. He pauses, wipes the man's arm, cleans the area, and looks up. "It's also rude to ignore her when she is speaking to you."

Ky blinks.

Dereck walks back nervously. "Him too," Ky says to Dereck, motioning to the man in the chair with Manny.

Manny whispers something to the man in the chair. The man gets up so Manny can cover the area and tape it off.

When the man leaves, Manny glances at Dereck. "Head home. I'll call you later."

I'm shocked Dereck doesn't protest, leaving him alone with Ky, and just walks out. The man in the suit locks the entrance and turns off the Open sign, making me nervous. Fear grips me when Ky walks toward the private room and opens the door, flicking on the light.

"Bring your shit," Ky demands in a hard tone. "Black ink and some red."

Manny grabs his tattoo gun and all his supplies. "If you wanted a tattoo, you could have asked nicely."

Ky gestures for me to come over. "What's going on?" I ask sarcastically.

He nods to the men behind me, and one of them grips me by the arm. "What the fuck?"

Manny steps forward. "Hurt her, and I'll kill you both," he warns, looking at the men.

Ky chuckles, clapping his hands. "How noble of you."

"Please, Ky. Don't hurt him," I plead as I enter the room.

"Please, Ky. Don't hurt him," he mocks. "How cute. I'm going to hurt him... just not how you think." Ky steps forward, sliding his hand between my thighs, making my breath hitch in my throat. "You're pussy, is hot. I bet it aches to be fucked."

He isn't wrong, and I hate him for it. There are times I play with myself in the shower remembering how he fucked me. How his cock filled me. How he made me feel. Like, I was everything.

He closes the door, and I'm alone with Ky and Manny. I fidget nervously. Manny leans with his back against the wall like this is normal.

"Lay on the table, Rubi," Ky says, rolling up the sleeves revealing tattoos and corded forearms.

Manny's eyes are trained on me. Watching me with hooded eyes as I hop up to face him. I contemplated running out screaming, but I saw the stars on the men outside guarding the door. The same stars on Ky's tattoo. They're Italian. He mentioned the men that work for his grandfather. I don't stand a chance of running away if I tried.

"Take off her pants."

My head whips toward Ky. "No!" I cry.

He nods toward Manny, and I watch as he straightens. "Manny?"

"He's not going to hurt you, princess. This is all about me."

"Not necessarily. This is about the truth." Ky leans in, rubbing his nose on my cheek. "I wouldn't be a good friend if I didn't tell you the truth, Rubi."

I pull away. "What are you talking about?"

Manny pulls his shirt over his head. His body is ripped. Lean with tattoos all over his skin similar to Ky's, and then I see it on his inner bicep. The same marking belonging to Ky's grandfather's family. He is one of them.

"I would like you to meet my half-brother. Manny Mancini. My father already had a child before he married my mother and had me."

I watch in horror as the puzzle pieces begin to fit. Manny lied. That is why he showed up. He was brought here because of me. Dereck is not his brother like he claimed. He lied. They all lied.

"You're all a bunch of liars," I seethe.

"I didn't lie." Ky points to Manny. "He did. I was handling things, and he couldn't help himself. Isn't that right, brother?"

Manny's eyes soften, but I look away. "Don't. It wasn't like that, Rubi. I was here to protect you."

"You couldn't get her a better job? Really, Pizza Hut." Ky shakes his head, looking at the ceiling dramatically.

"It's close by. What was I supposed to do?"

"She hates Pizza Hut for a reason," Ky scolds.

Pfft. "How the hell should I know she hated it. It was short notice."

"Are you listening to yourselves? You two are fucking crazy. Insane."

I'm about to hop off, but Ky moves between my legs. "Where are you going? We're not finished."

I try to move, but he pins me, and before I know it, he is dragging my pants off along with my thong. "What are you doing, Ky!" I screech.

I stopped moving.

My cheeks flame.

I'm exposed, dressed in nothing but a bra and sweater. If I move my legs, Manny and Ky will see my shaved pussy.

"Now, for the fun part."

"Leave her alone, Ky," Manny warns.

"Nah, brother. I need you to do something for me first since you were inclined to cover me up. I appreciate the red tulip. A symbol of the Mancini women." My eyes widen, looking at Manny.

"It was to protect you," Manny says helplessly.

I shake my head, feeling so stupid. That is why he pointed out the letters in the cafeteria at school. He marked me.

"I hate you. Both of you."

Ky pushes my legs wider. "You don't hate me. You need me. Like I need you, but first, we need to fix what you did."

My nostrils flare when he stares at my wet slit licking his lips. "What are you talking about?"

Ky takes a step back. "Eat her pussy."

Manny's eyes fill with lust. "I can't." But I see that he wants to, and I panic.

"No."

Ky nods. "Yeah. He's dying to have you, but he knows he can't. That's his punishment for touching you. For branding you without my consent." Ky swipes my clit with his finger earning a whimper from my traitorous throat. "Make her come."

"What are you doing, Ky?"

"You thought it was him this morning." Guilt clenches inside me. "I'm going to watch you come on his tongue, knowing he can't stick his cock in you. There is nothing worse than tasting something you can't have. Then watching me fuck you when he's done." His thumb rubs my clit, making my ass squirm on the black leather chaise. "You have the heads of the Mancini mafia wrapped around your pussy, Rubi."

Manny settles between my legs, and I look at Ky, pleading with my eyes for him to stop this, but he doesn't. My mouth parts when Manny swipes his tongue over my clit.

"Fuck," Manny growls between my thighs. "She tastes so good." The vibration from his throat caused my hips to grind brazenly. He mauls me with his tongue, and a moan escapes my throat with every flick.

Ky closes the distance and frees his cock stroking it slowly from base to tip. "Suck my cock, *principessa*. I want to feel your moans."

Oh my God. I don't think his big cock would fit in my mouth. I lick my lips, and he pushes the head inside. A little bit at first, so my mouth can adjust. He knows it's my first time.

I lick and suck, imagining it's a lollipop. "Fuck, just like that," he says breathlessly.

I smile, and then his hand twists in my hair, gripping the strands as he sinks deeper. Manny swirls his tongue, and I gasp, holding on to Ky's shaft with one hand and Manny's head in the other.

Manny looks up with my pussy between his lips. I moan at how good it feels.

It's dirty and hot.

I feel sexy when Manny grips his hands on my hips, holding me like I'm the most delicious thing he's ever tasted, and he can't get enough. Ky's hand cups my face under my jaw, caressing my cheek with his thumb while he fucks my mouth. The salty taste of him fills my mouth while my climax builds.

I gasp. "Mm....."

"She's going to come," Ky says fucking my mouth. "So am I." His cock swells, my lips feeling the hard ridges and veins on his shaft. Drool slides down my chin. Tears pool in my eyes every time he hits the back of my throat. "Take it. Relax your throat." I do. "You're perfect, you know that? You're so fucking beautiful it hurts."

He grunts.

I moan.

When Manny fucks me with his tongue, in and out. Faster and faster. I push his head so I can feel him deeper. He sucks my clit just right, and I come hard on a scream.

"Yes. Mm...."

"Shit," Ky growls, and he comes down my throat. Our eyes meet, and I'm lost in him. "There's my girl."

Manny sucks my pussy, drinking my arousal. It's too much, and my legs begin to shake. He pulls out, making a sucking noise. His mouth is wet, dripping down his chin.

His tongue darts out. "You're fucking delicious." He glances at Ky. "She's sweet."

"I know. Now move and prep the gun."

"Why?"

"You'll see."

Ky is between my legs, pulling me close to the edge of the chaise. He shoves his cock inside me in one go. I gasp at his size, forgetting how big he is. "You're mine," he rasps. "Say it," he commands, holding me by the waist with his hands.

Manny is watching Ky fuck me. His brown eyes are so dark they are almost black. My eyes drop to the bulge in his jeans. He's hard while his hand preps the tattoo gun. I'm wondering why Ky wants him to have it ready.

Ky holds himself up with his hand flat on the leather by my head, looking down at where we are joined. "Say you're mine."

He feels so good. I can't help it. I'll always be his, no matter what. It doesn't matter how hard I try. He won't let it. He consumed me since the day I met him.

Every waking moment.

Every sleepless hour.

I dream of him.

He pushes deeper, and I swear I can feel him in my lower belly. I grip his hard shoulders and caress his face. "I'm yours." He smiles.

He fucks me slowly, not caring that Manny is in the room. He fades away, and it's just us. We're back in his yard, surrounded by grass and planted daisies.

I can still smell the grass and the crisp air of fall as summer ends. "We're going to be together forever, Rubi. Always. You're my favorite girl. My best friend."

Tears sting the corner of my eyes. His face blurs, and I hear him whisper, "You're my favorite girl. Always." He's remembering the same moment, and I know we were always meant to be.

Words escape my lips. "I love you." I come on a gasp, and he soon follows, spilling inside me. When he pulls out, his mask settles in place. He tucks himself away, and reality hits me. Where I am and who I'm with.

Ky cleans me with a wet towel, and my eyes fly to Manny. His expression is dark, but I feel embarrassed and scared when Ky walks over to inspect my pussy. His fingers slide over the top part where I shave.

"I need you to tattoo my name here," he points to Manny.

"Ky, no. Stop messing around."

His eyes flick up. "You're pussy is mine. He covered over my name. Now he gets to brand what he wants with my name."

I shake my head. "That's crazy, Ky."

"Rubi"--he smiles manically-- "I am crazy." He looks to Manny. "Do it, or they will hold her down, and I'll do it myself. Ky Mancini, with black and red letters. Make sure it looks pretty, brother. I want to look at it while I come all over it."

He wouldn't. Manny wouldn't do it. My stomach drops when he sits in the chair with his supplies on a tray and rolls over. His face was right there in front of my pussy. He puts on a pair of gloves and squirts solution on a paper towel.

"I hate you," I grit. "I hate you for doing this. You don't have to do it."

Ky smiles, leaning on the wall and watching. This was his surprise.

Manny wipes the area I shaved like an idiot. "He's next in line to the Mancini mafia dynasty, and I'm his right hand. You belong to us, Rubi. If he wants it, I have to do it. The flower I tattooed on your arm is for your protection. I protected you because he ordered me to, and I'm glad he did. Please don't fight us." He preps the ink. "It's pointless. He took his birthright to save you, and I would have done the same." I look away, gritting my teeth at the sting. "Relax, I'll make it look good. I promise."

Ky pushes off the wall and caresses my hair. "The tulip is for your protection, but this is for me." He leans, kisses my temple, and whispers something in Italian. "*Regina.*"

CHAPTER TWENTY-SEVEN
Ky

SHE LOVES ME. I saw it in her eyes when I was inside her. But I had to prove a point with the tattoo on her pussy. It hurt like hell when I saw she erased me, and it was my half-brother who was falling for her that did it. It felt like my shattered heart was being hammered into a million pieces.

I wanted to punish him and remind her who she belongs to. Me. She's mine. I know it. He knows it. Now everyone will know it.

"You think that was a good idea?" Manny asks outside of the spa so she can have her hair and nails done for the first time.

"I do."

"Bullying her to love you isn't the best strategy."

"Neither is letting my idiot brother fuck my girl."

He chuckles. "You left, and when I took her to eat after the tattoo, we ran into your exes."

"What?"

"Yeah, cheerleaders," he scoffs. "She thinks they hold a candle to her, you know. Not the best way to get the girl." He says, makes quotation marks with his fingers.

"Fuck," I mutter.

"What?"

"She's going to open her mouth and it's going to get back to her father that she's still around if he doesn't know already."

"We keep an eye on her, but running is stupid. You know that. She wants to finish school, and ripping her away will make things

229

worse. It's bad enough we're in public school when there is a perfectly good prep school less than four miles away."

"Too close to home. You know that."

"I get it. So now what?"

"Nothing. I come here."

He raises a brow. "You...in public school?"

"My father doesn't care if I graduate now that I will take over when my grandfather steps down. My father fucked up in my grandfather's eyes with your mother and mine, so that leaves us."

"How are you going to get in? There are only four months left of school, and we have to take care of her father."

"I know. I'll transfer in as a Mancini and wait until he shows up. I have enough credits to graduate."

"Then what?"

"I'll kill him."

Manny scratches his cheek, lost in thought. "Was she close to him?"

I shake my head. "No, but I know she had hope like every kid with one living parent. It doesn't matter who you came from or what your parents are or weren't. You always try to look for love in your parents. Even if they're shit. They could be mafia kings, an addict, or a total fuck up. You look for some type of fucked up love hoping they will give it to you someday."

"That's bullshit. Not all of us are that lucky."

I know he means our father and the shitty upbringing he had with his single mother living in Ohio, milking every penny my father sent to her for him behind my mother's back. When I found out about him, I knew what my father said about women was total bullshit. He left Manny's mom and married mine, not caring if she had his kid. She didn't walk out on him like my mother, but she wasn't the best either. She was in it for the money. But Rubi is different. I'm different. We all come from something fucked up, and not everything is perfect.

"Are the supplies delivered to the house?"

He laughs through his nose. "Yeah."

"Fuck you, it's important."

"I know." He looks down at his feet. "Don't fuck it up this time."

I shove him playfully. "I won't."

I always wanted a sibling, but I had Rubi, and she was all I ever needed, but it doesn't hurt to have a brother.

"What about her brother?"

"I need to take her to see him. He wants to see her."

"Isn't there another guy that's part of your little circle? Chris. Don't you want to loop him in?"

"You mean the one that tried to do the same and take out my girl on a date?"

He angles his head. "Yeah, fuck him. We don't need to tell him shit."

"That's what I thought."

The door opens, and Rubi steps out. Her strawberry-blonde hair flowing like a silk curtain. My chest tightens, remembering the day I first saw her; she looks like an angel. Her nails are manicured and polished, the color of marshmallows. Her pretty toes match her nails in the designer sandals I brought for her from Italy.

She beams. "I'm ready."

———

"Why are we here?" Rubi asks.

I look down at her feet. "Are your feet dry?"

She nods, and I hand her a pair of designer boots. She takes them, waiting for me to tell her why we are in the parking at a prison.

"Your brother wants to see you." She doesn't protest and slides on the boots after I hand her a pair of socks.

The back door opens by the security detail my grandfather insisted I have for our safety.

Manny is waiting for us to follow. "Is he okay?" She rushes out. "I've been wanting to ask but know the circumstances. I want to talk to Abby, to Noah..."

"Just him, Rubi. For now."

The two men follow Manny, waiting at the entrance, and I sit in the waiting area for her to come out when she is done speaking to her brother. He wants to tell her himself that he has nothing to do with his father wanting to kill her.

I met with him and told him my plan. What I've done. He knew there was something more to my behavior. Something I kept hidden from everyone. I'm Ky Mancini, heir to the Mancini family, and Rubiana is my queen.

CHAPTER TWENTY-EIGHT
Rubi

TEARS well up in my eyes when Tyler walks in dressed in an orange jumpsuit handcuffed. The cuffs make noise when he walks, and he notices he also has them on his ankles.

He sits at the table across from me, and I look around to find the correction officers watching us. My eyes meet his, and I see remorse, anger, and guilt.

"Hi."

He smiles, but I can tell nothing is happy about his expression. "Hey." He leans on the metal table, lowering his voice. "I'm sorry."

I nod, but my stomach churns, noticing that he shaved his head and he's... broken. This is not the brother I met for the first time. This is a man fighting his demons in a pit of hell with no one to talk to.

"I know," I respond.

"Are you okay?"

"Yeah, I guess I am. So far. How... are you?"

"Fucked. This place is not for the weak heart. There are some bad people here, and the only thing I could do is survive. It is why I'm shackled like this from defending myself. Ky is trying to get the lawyers to get me out on good behavior, but it's hard when every time you try to take a piss, they are trying to break you."

He means they try to screw you to see if you're soft. If you break. But I can't tell him not to fight.

"You fight," I tell him. I know it's wrong to say since he knows how to defend himself, but I can't stand it if something

235

happens to him. "You hear me? Don't let them hurt you. You can go back to school and finish."

"I will, but it's not because I want to... I have my reasons."

I lean back. He wants to right a wrong, but I ask anyway.

"Why?"

"I have nothing to lose. Stephen left the house. My mother is all alone, and she's not well. I need you to stay away. Don't visit her because he knows you will go see her. I know she is not your mother, but you have a good heart, Rubi. My father is an asshole, and I'm not going to let him fuck with my mother. You and Mom are the only thing I have left. I don't want the company. I don't want anything he has built. He's a monster. Not a father. He knew where you were the whole time. He knew about your mother and stepfather. They were all using you."

"I know."

I suspected. I knew there was more, and nothing was a coincidence. I jumped the right fence at the right time, even if I paid the price, but Ky saved me. He's protecting me; if I ask him, he would keep Tyler, too.

"I know what I did was messed up, but someone set me up. They sent me pictures of Abby and Noah. Someone knew I would lose it. How I felt about her."

I pinch my brows. " Who?"

He shakes his head. "I don't know. That is why I need to go back to West Lake Prep. I can only think it was someone who knew Abby. Someone she confided in or someone that is close friends with Noah."

"Don't do anything stupid that will land you back in here."

"I won't. Not with who my sister is with."

"Still, Tyler. What you're planning is dangerous. Stephen is out there; no one can touch him because of his business. Too much is at stake," I say softly.

"I know. But promise me," he pleads. His eyes begging. "Whatever Ky wants, go along with it. Let him take over our side of the business. He knows what to do. He's smart. Clever"––he smiles—"he loves you, Rubi. He loves you so much. He's good underneath his madness. He's good. Remember that."

I blink back the sting. "I will."

A buzzing noise echoes in the room.

"Times up," the officer announces.

Tyler gets up, and I want to cry. "Don't come back here. Promise me."

"I will."

"I'm glad you're my sister. I love you, Rubi."

Tears slide down my cheeks. "I love you, too. Brother." I watch him leave with my heart in my throat.

I walk out and shield my eyes with my hand from the afternoon sun. "You, okay?" Ky asks.

I sniff. "No. My brother is in there, and someone obviously set him up."

"He'll be out. I talked to people on the inside to look out for him. He's tough. Thank God we trained together."

"We're two hours away, and I put money in his account. I'll visit him every week."

"Thank you.

"You can write to him, but I'll send him the letters. It's risky if you send it through the mail. I don't trust Stephen. He's been around my father too long, and he knows people. People in high places."

"What about Caroline?"

"I'll pay her bills, but I can't do much about Tyler's truck. It's under Stephen's name. I'll buy him a new one for his birthday when he gets out."

I snort. "Show off."

The next week at school, I'm sitting in class listening to the teacher lecturing us on career choices and how they can impact the future when the door opens. The teacher stops talking and turns to see who walked in. Ky hands him a slip, his eyes landing on me.

"Transfer student. Welcome, Ky Mancini," he says, pronouncing it wrong.

"Mancini," Ky corrects him.

"Sorry."

"It's okay. We all make mistakes," Ky replies, earning him laughs from the room.

He walks down the aisle, getting appreciative glances from the girls. The guy seated next to me, Tomas, with his nerdy glasses that make his eyes look like an owl, shifts nervously in his seat.

"Go find another seat," Ky tells him.

"S-sure." Tomas grabs his pencils and notebook like his life depended on it.

Ky takes his seat and pushes his desk, closing the space. The teacher, Mr. Levine, is about to object, but Ky beats him to it.

"So I can catch up on what I missed."

Mr. Levine opens and closes his mouth but nods. "Yeah, good idea."

Ky turns and smiles, showing me his perfect white teeth. "Miss me?"

A blush creeps up my neck, and I grin. "Maybe."

———

"Come here," Ky whispers behind me after third period.

I close my locker, noticing that everyone avoids getting in his way through the rumbling crowd. He follows me everywhere I go and is in most of my classes but the last one. I'm not sure about the others.

He reaches for my hand and tugs me along when he sees I'm not following him.

"Where…"

I don't get to finish. He pushes me inside the janitor's closet and locks the door.

He grabs my ass and pushes me forward so I can feel how hard his cock is through his jeans. "How did you transfer here?" I ask, trying not to look desperate, wanting him to sink inside me.

"I used the address to the house, and technically, I have enough credits to graduate. I'm here because of you. I don't want to be away from you anymore." His eyes skate toward the band of my comfy leggings. "I need you right now."

I smile. "But...I have class."

"So do I, but I can't walk around school with a huge ass boner knowing my girl is inside a class somewhere."

I look around the dim closet full of paper towels and toilet paper that gets stuck on your ass when you wipe yourself, realizing this is crazy. But I can't help myself.

I hear myself say, "Okay."

He slides his hand down my panties cautiously. He remembers that I have the tattoo, and it's almost healed, but I haven't been able to have sex. He slept in my room every night since he got back from visiting his grandfather. He takes me out to eat and plays with Hope. I think the cat likes him more than I do now.

I feel the cold air on the heated skin of my ass when he slides my panties down my hips and hear him undo his pants. "Turn around and face the wall with your palms facing up."

When I do, I feel his warm breath fanning my cheek. "I've been dying to sink my fat cock inside you, Rubi. I can't take not being inside you another minute." The tip of his cock nudges my entrance. He goes slow at first. He wraps his fingers around my neck and then shoves inside me. We both groan at the tight fit. "Fuck, you're so tight. You looked so pretty when I walked into class today. I can't help myself. I need you."

"I love you," I cry out.

He places his hand over my mouth to stifle my moans as he fucks me. "I love you, Rubi," he rasps against the side of my neck, causing tiny hairs to stand on the back of my neck. "Give me that tight pussy."

CHAPTER TWENTY-NINE
Rubi

I'M SEATED in the cafeteria at my usual table with Manny on Friday at lunch. The doors open, and there is a hush around the cafeteria when Ky walks in.

"Show off," Manny mutters to my right.

"You know how he likes to make an entrance."

His, dark jeans hang low, showing the band of his boxers. He fills out his black shirt, revealing his lean muscles. My favorite part is his biceps, where they bulge slightly when he flexes his arms. I also love his black hair that matches his eyes.

"He loves when you stare at him like that."

"Stare at him like what?" I ask.

"Like he walked the fucking moon or some shit."

"He did. My moon."

"No, he made me write his name on your..."

"Shh..." Manny smiles. "That's a secret."

"It tasted good."

"Stop it. He will hear you."

"So, he told me too."

"Told you to do what," Ky says, kissing my cheek and rubbing his nose like he does with Hope.

"Eat," Manny replies, holding his gaze.

"That was to torture you."

"It worked," he admits, making me blush.

"You two look so cute together," Katie says, walking up with her tray and taking a seat.

"Way to rub it in," Manny mumbles, giving me a wink.

241

"He'll survive."

Manny points his straw at Ky. "That works. If I survive, I get her."

"What..."

Ky interjects. "Family stuff. Rules."

Did he just say that I belong to Manny if something happens to Ky?

"But what if Manny has a..."

"Comes second," Manny interjects.

"Whatever you guys are talking about doesn't matter. You two look amazing together," Katie says, her expression softening.

Cesar has to see that she is crazy about him, but he won't do anything.

"After school, meet me in the front, not the student parking lot," Ky says, picking up soggy French fries from my plate.

"Why?"

"Less attention," Manny answers for him.

"Okay."

It would look weird if a black SUV with suited bodyguards waiting for us in the student parking lot on this side of town. It's bad enough Ky draws attention when he walks into a room. Manny is better at hiding it with his friendly demeanor and is more low-key. Ky has that don't fuck with me attitude.

When the bell rings, I rush through the crowded hallway toward the front of the school in the opposite direction. People are trying to head to the bus or get to their ride.

When I open the doors, the sun's glare causes my vision to darken for a minute. I didn't see the hands grab me or hear anyone. I'm lifted roughly off the ground and shoved into the back of a van. I try to scream, knowing there is nothing I can do. Someone hits me on the head with something hard, and everything goes dark.

———

I wake up with a gasp. My eyes go wide, trying to see, but it's dark, and I can't make out a wall. I'm naked. I look up, and my arms are tied with rope to hooks bolted to the ceiling. It smells damp and musty. My neck aches from hanging forward. I don't know how long I was out. I wince when the pain radiates from my head from where they hit me. I want to scream, but if I do, someone will come, and I can't fight them off.

Tears slide down my chin. I look at my feet, and there is dried blood on the floor, probably from the previous person they killed or tortured. I'm hoping Ky will find me in time.

A door opens, and dread squeezes my throat. The sound coming from somewhere behind me. My arms begin to shake. Terror claws up my spine when I hear footsteps getting closer.

"You're awake." A man with metal-rimmed glasses comes into view. He turns on a light above me. I'm in a warehouse and guessing the abandoned ones on the border by West Park and West Lake.

I take a ragged breath. "How long have I been out?"

"A day."

"Are you... going to kill me?"

That is why I'm here, and these men were sent by Stephen.

"After we rape you, yes. Even if you survive, they wouldn't want you so...damaged."

"Fuck you," I spit, holding back the tears with the way his eyes are trained on my breasts.

"That's the plan. There are three of us. Let's see if you can take us at the same time. I don't mind a little damaged flesh. I like my meat well done."

"You're a pig. Who sent you?"

I know the answer, but I want to hear it from him. I want to know if there is someone else involved that would like me dead.

"Daddy dearest. He wants to cut off loose ends." He smiles maliciously. "You're...the loose end."

The door opens, and two men walk in, and I panic. "Please. Don't do this. If you want to kill me, just do it."

The man with glasses laughs, and so do the other two men.

They are big. Muscled with shaved heads. One with blue jeans runs the palm of his hand over the bulge in his jeans, but the other keeps looking at my arm. The one with the red tulip and the daises.

"She's...branded.."

The man with glasses turns his head. "And."

"Do you know what they will do to us? They will slaughter our families, our parents, our children. I don't think this is a good idea. I don't want any part of it."

"Then you'll watch while we take her. She looks good, and I want a piece of her."

The guy steps back and shakes his head. "No. Let her go."

"Hell, no." The man rubbing at his cock says.

"Please. I left. I don't want anything my father wants. He doesn't understand."

"Shut your mouth," The man with glasses says in a hard tone.

"But..." He slaps me across the face. Pain hits me like a brick pounding in my skull. Heat radiates over my cheek. My face feels like I'm on fire. My limbs are aching and sore.

I hear a loud boom but can't see from my left eye. Something warm drips down the right side of my face, and then loud voices followed by gunshots echo around the room. A loud ringing sound blares in my head. I feel hands on my skin, and I scream.

"Shh... it's me, baby. It's Ky." I sag in relief, and I feel something soft and warm. "Get me a blanket! Manny, call the doctor. She's hurt!" He pauses. "Now!" He roars. "I got you, Rubi. I'm sorry. I'm so sorry." His voice is hoarse from screaming, and I feel the panic and relief coming off him.

"You came. You came," I repeat, but my head feels fuzzy, and the floor feels like it flew to the ceiling. Everything goes black.

CHAPTER THIRTY

Ky

Four Months Later

THE TWINKLING LIGHTS float above us under the cool sky. Spring is in the air, and the daisies sway in the wind.

"Tyler should be out soon,' I tell her, playing with her hair on my lap. "He can start school this coming year."

"He's changed, hasn't he?"

"He's not the same Tyler we once knew, but he'll be alright."

"No word on my father?"

"Not yet. But don't worry." I look over at the five-bodyguard roaming the property, knowing they are the best. My father wants nothing but the best for us. I'm learning the business with Manny. We went to Italy after graduation, and she met my grandfather. He said I did good and that she was perfect. That she was beautiful. He surprised us with a small wedding. We were married in Sicily, with the sun setting on the horizon.

"I'm not. I trust you," she says, and my chest fills with pride.

I don't want her to worry. Tyler wants to handle his father. He wants me to make sure Rubi is okay.

"How are you feeling?" I ask.

She looks down at the small bump in her stomach with a smile. "I feel better. The nausea has subsided."

247

"I brought crackers and water." I pull out a pack of crackers and a bottle of sparkling water, ensuring she has everything she needs. There is nothing I wouldn't do for her.

"Thank you, but I would like a chocolate shake." She sighs. "But I don't want to leave. I love it out here." She looks up at the lights. "It's beautiful."

I built her a treehouse in the backyard where we first met. I planted fresh daisies and a row of Tulips.

After they took her, I located her at the warehouses from a tracker I planted in her bag and on her phone. The idiots dropped her bag right outside the warehouse, and it didn't take long to figure out where she was. I had the doctor treat her head wound and run tests because she almost passed out again. He ruled out a concussion and found that she was pregnant. She was dehydrated but said she would be fine with IV fluids.

I send a text. "It's coming."

"What is," she asks, plucking a daisy.

"Two chocolate shakes."

She smiles, holding up a daisy. "Ready?"

"You already know the answer. I love you, Rubi. You're my girl. Always."

I reach inside the bag I brought and grab the note I wrote for her, waiting until this moment to give it to her. In the backyard, behind the house, we met under our tree house with her favorite daisies.

"I wrote something for you."

She looks up, and I see surprise in her pretty eyes when she takes it from me. My gaze lands on her belly, knowing our child is growing inside her. She opens the notebook paper like the one she left me all those years ago when we were eleven. But this time, it isn't a goodbye. It isn't filled with things we wish we could confess but with something I needed to say...something she deserved to know.

"You keep spoiling me, Ky. You didn't have to write me a note on paper. I love you. I love us." My gaze lands on her belly, knowing our child is growing inside. A child we will both love and never leave.

I place my hand gently over her heart to feel it beating when she begins to read, and I wait.

Rubi

Sometimes, I'm afraid I'll wake up and find that this is all a dream, but I pinch myself and look in the mirror to see the slight swell of my belly, knowing that it's real. That Ky loves me, and I love him. I feel safe as his wife, wrapped in his arms, protected by the storm in his gaze.

I settle in his lap. He places his hand over my chest where my heart beats, and I hold the paper in the light...and begin.

To my wife Rubi,

True love never ends.

Because days don't exist in forever.

It is there when we think it isn't.

Because it holds on without letting go.

It is a love that is carved into the soul.

A love I refuse to let go.

Because we are connected.

It doesn't matter if we get lost along the way.

We always find our way back to each other.

To continue what we started, so I can take your breath and give you mine knowing you are never alone and that I love you.

We can sit under the stars with the daisies you love so much swaying in the wind sharing something beautiful. Our Love.

Love, *Ky*

The End.
Thank you for reading Ky and Rubi's story I hope you enjoyed
He Loves Me.
Look out for Tyler and Abby's story
She loves me/ She loves me not

ABOUT THE AUTHOR

Carmen

Rosales is an emerging Latinx author of Steamy, and Dark Romance. She loves spending time with her family. When she is not writing, she is reading. She is an Army veteran and is currently completing her Doctorate Degree in Business and has the love and support of her husband and five children. She also writes under Delilah Croww for her DARK romance horror stories with really dark themes that is coming out soon.

Join her VIP list- https://carmenrosales.com/ and https://delilahcroww.com

She loves to see a review and interact with her readers.

Scan the QR code to follow her on Social Media and sign up for her Newsletter:

www.ingramcontent.com/pod-product-compliance
Lightning Source LLC
Chambersburg PA
CBHW030722060525
26195CB00028B/454